Twelve Nights Box Set

A REGENCY HOLIDAY ROMANCE DUET

TWELVE NIGHTS

CARRIE LOMAX

Copyright © 2019-2024 by Carrie Lomax

All rights reserved.

No part of this book may be reproduced in any form or by any electronic or mechanical means, including information storage and retrieval systems, without written permission from the author, except for the use of brief quotations in a book review.

This book may not be used to train any Large Language Model database or otherwise used in any artificial intelligence program without the express written permission of the author. No platform has the right to sublicense others to reproduce and/or otherwise use this work in any manner for purposes of training artificial intelligence technologies to generate text without the author's specific and express permission.

This is a work of fiction. All characters, events, and most locations are invented by the author; any resemblance to actual people, places and events are typically coincidental, except actual place names such as cities and countries.

ASIN: B0BMSJHW1M

e-ISBN: 9798215773697

Print ISBN: 9798341076358

About the Twelve Nights Duet

The Twelve Nights Regency Christmas novellas follow two cousins who are opposites and best friends.

Amity is a country mouse, quiet and reserved, while Holly is a city girl with a sparkling wit and capricious whims. Holly's greatest aim is to make a brilliant match with a handsome, titled man. In Amity's book, *Twelve Nights of Scandal*, she is expected to receive an offer of marriage from Finlay Weston, Amity's brother's best friend.

When that plan falls through, Holly falls back on her wits and wiles to charm an inappropriate bachelor…and soon finds herself publicly disgraced. To set things right, her exasperated parents arrange for her to marry a stoic soldier Holly has never met, Rey Sharp. They are as opposite as can be. Can they overcome their differences and commit to true love in *Twelve Nights of Ruin*?

You'll find both stories included in this box set. Download & start reading today.

Twelve Nights of Scandal

BOOK 1

Chapter One

CHRISTMAS, 1816

"I refuse to wear old bed linens to Uncle Foster's Christmas house party." Amity Mayweather had standards, and they did not include dancing in bedclothes. Her mother cast her an exasperated glare. A pebble of guilt formed inside Amity's chest. Nonetheless, Amity crossed her arms over her bosoms and raised one eyebrow. Then, her chin.

"I could send Mary Anne instead," Mrs. Mayweather mused casually. With the broad sheet of fabric as wide as her arms, she matched the corners and folded it neatly in half. "She has at least one proper gown. Your green one could be made over if we add several inches—"

"Your best chance of seeing one of us wed is to send Letty," Amity cut her mother off. Her third-youngest sister had all the beauty in the family. Amity judged her own appearance passable. Her best features were a creamy complexion, dark eyes and even teeth, but her brown hair refused to hold a curl on the rare occasions she had to attempt making one. Her late-adolescent growth had brought with it bosoms, even if she couldn't fill out a bodice the way her youngest sister, Charity, could. At sixteen, Charity might have been regarded as more attractive if her wide eyes were not offset by an equally large mouth, which she exercised to great length—a trait the family hoped she might yet outgrow. Mary Anne, the second-oldest sister, was as tall as a giraffe and about as graceful, thanks to nearsightedness. But Leticia possessed all the sisters' best qualities combined. An enviable complexion, tall, willowy figure, and doe eyes the color of spring ferns. Thanks to Mr. Mayweather and her brother Ellis's untimely death, Letty's beauty was the sum total any of the women had to recommend them in marriage.

"You are the oldest," Mrs. Mayweather replied thoughtfully. "As well as the only girl who hasn't had a new dress since..." Her voice hitched. "We can turn your green wool to freshen it and add new cuffs."

In the years since the Mayweathers had lost Amity's father and brother in a single afternoon, their station in life had taken a steep dive into penury. Although her mother's jointure gave the family the right to live on the premises of Wells House, the mansion where Mrs. Mayweather had once been mistress, an acrimonious disharmony between Anne and her brother-in-law had made the relationship unpalatable. The new Mayweather occupants—Amity's uncle and aunt—so desired for their newly dependent relative to remarry that they had all but placed the grieving widow in a halter and marched her around the town square to be rid of her. Mrs. Mayweather had been so offended by her brother- and sister-in-law's meddling that she'd moved the family of five women to Kearny, a tiny village on the edge of Hertfordshire and Essex. Though charming on a bright afternoon, there was little to recommend the village beyond inexpensive property to let.

Amity dropped her arms. "I can fit into Charity's red

velvet if it isn't too moth-eaten." She and her youngest sister were of a similar height.

"There, you see? One red, one green, one white, and your best blue dress with the yellow ribbons at the bodice. Enough for a fortnight of visiting. The blue will be perfect for a Twelfth Night ball." Mrs. Mayweather spoke with a certain determination, a hardness that belied her cheerful words. "It is kind of Mr. and Mrs. Mayweather," she said, meaning Amity's uncle and aunt, a common confusion in such a large family. "So few families are hosting this year on account of the poor harvest."

The year had been horribly cold. Crop failures had hit Kearny with the force of a battering ram. Amity, Mary Anne, Leticia and Charity had borne the transition from well-tutored young ladies to penny-hoarding tenders of chickens and reluctant gardeners with relative equanimity. But this year, the women had been hard-pressed to figure out how to scrape together edible meals as their egg money dwindled. They had been forced to sacrifice members of their flock to the stew pot.

"You can't cut up your last set of good bedsheets, mother," Amity chided.

"Only one," her mother insisted softly, eyeing the long fall of pristine white linen. "There are two in a set, and cases as well. There will still be enough for the first girl to marry. The lot of you are taking your time about it, if I am honest."

Whoever married first was to receive the contents of Mrs. Mayweather's trunk as a wedding gift. It contained everything they had saved from their comfortable old life and had avoided selling to get them through the lean years. One quilt. Two goose down blankets so light and soft and warm that pulling them out of the chest had become Amity's favorite winter ritual. A warm plaid shawl, a gift from a long-forgotten friend of Mrs. Mayweather's, carefully maintained for each winter.

Christening gowns. A silver baby bowl and spoon. These objects had been invested with their most heartfelt dreams. It was imperative that whichever Mayweather girl married first, she married well enough to earn these precious gifts.

Amity held no delusions that it could be her.

She watched the long column of her mother's neck work as she swallowed. Finding suitable marriage prospects might have been easier had the Mayweathers confessed the degree of their poverty to their relatives. Their ability to purchase things like fabric for new gowns, or gloves, or ribbons for the bonnets they tried to repair by weaving straw into the holes, could have been alleviated by a few coins from their wealthier relatives had Mrs. Mayweather been inclined to ask.

"I shall try to find a husband at the house party," Amity replied with a lump in her throat. Luxuries like love and romance were well out of her budget.

"All I want is for my eldest—" Amity did not miss the hesitation in her mother's voice, for her brother, Ellis, had been older by one year, "—daughter to enjoy this visit with her favorite cousin."

Amity grinned. "Holly won't care how I dress, Mum. Save your bed sheets. Seeing Holly is the greatest gift I could ask for this Christmas."

❋

Snowflakes as fat as goose feathers floated down from the bright winter sky to dissolve on Amity's cheeks. Beneath the fur sleigh blanket she was almost too warm. A brick at her feet made sweat dampen the double layers of stockings in her worn but sturdy boots. Her breath fogged the cold air.

"It's been so long since I've seen you," her cousin said,

squeezing her gloved hand. Holly's infectious smile revealed even white teeth above a plump lower lip. Her fair hair had been curled into ringlets that bounced as the horse pulled them over fresh snowfall. All Amity could think about during the long journey was how little she deserved this and how much it had cost her mother to send her such a distance. Once, it would have been nothing, but those days were gone. Tucked deep pocket were a handful of coins, Amity's share of the egg money.

"I saved every letter," Amity said, squeezing back. "Such as it was."

Holly laughed, a tinkling sound injurious to Amity's ears. Holly had the means to write often. Amity did not. She stretched her money by saving odd scraps of paper and writing on them with chicken feathers sharpened into quills. Proper writing quills were hardened to hold a sharp point between trimmings. The backyard variety left blots across her missives that rendered portions of Amity's letters nearly illegible.

"You know me," Amity agreed with all the humor she could muster.

"Couldn't you have used a full sheet of paper?" Holly teased, not knowing how it cut. Amity focused on the bracing air and the jingle of the horse's tack, but her cousin continued. "You cannot be so busy in that little village that you must scratch notes upon any paper you find at hand."

"My thoughts run too fast to capture at once." Amity forced a laugh. In truth, she would give her right arm for a proper stack of writing paper. Amity pushed away the thought. The sleigh rounded a curve in the road. Her breath stilled as she waited for a glimpse of her childhood home… there. Past the trees, Wells House stood as it always had. Amity's heart expanded at the vista spread before her, timeless and grand. When she remembered herself, she asked, "How are you enjoying London?"

The rote question cost her nothing to ask. Amity had been on the cusp of her first season when her father and brother had died in a carriage accident. London remained indistinct in her imagination.

"I love it!" Holly clapped, before burying her gloved hands in the blankets. "The balls, the dancing, the theatre, it's all so medical. I wish you could be there, Amity. You would thrive."

They hit a bump and flew an inch off the leather seats. Amity's teeth clacked together when they landed. Holly laughed.

"Or go mad," Amity replied archly. Despite her denial a kernel of jealousy sprouted in her breast. Holly was living the life she might have had, if Amity's father or brother still had breath. Envy was a useless emotion, though, so Amity pushed it away. "My country sensibilities aren't suited to town life."

"Nonsense. I wish you were there with me. My father is pressing me to accept a suitor." Holly made a face. "Finlay Weston, believe it or not."

Amity's blood froze as if the carriage had taken an unexpected detour into the river. "Not my Finn?"

"No, not yours. Ellis's." Holly clapped a hand over her mouth. "Does it pain you to speak of your brother?"

"Of course not," Amity replied, distantly. She could talk of Ellis for hours. Her brother had been her best friend and constant playmate in the summers when he hadn't been at school. He had thought school boring, but Amity had longed for more than the simple lessons provided by the governess and, later, tutors, for the girls educated at home. She, Finn and Ellis had been inseparable every summer—whether the boys had welcomed her presence or not. "Is he coming, then?"

"Mr. Poker-arse?" Holly chortled. Amity cast her cousin a scandalized look. "He's not the boy you played with anymore. Mr. Weston is handsome, but he has no humor whatsoever."

Amity pasted a smile on. Finlay Weston wasn't the only one who had changed. In the three years since Amity had last seen her cousin and best friend, Holly had acquired a certain calculating affectedness that one might call "polish." She smiled too much and tossed her head coquettishly. Although she was more beautiful than ever, Amity liked her less than when they had been girls braiding one another's hair during infrequent visits to Wells House. Still, she was Amity's favorite cousin, and her presence at Wells House this Christmas was a privilege Amity was determined to enjoy.

The sleigh stopped before the great stone house, and Amity gazed up at the edifice that housed her happiest childhood memories. Sadness dragged at her heart. She wished Finlay Weston wasn't coming. There was no one in the world Amity would less rather see. He would remind her of how much everything had changed, and not for the better. That way lay self-pity. She straightened her shoulders.

"You must protect me from him," Holly whispered, gripping her hand hard enough to pinch Amity's fingers. "Stay by my side so Mr. Weston doesn't have an opportunity to offer for me."

"Aren't you worried that after a fourth season, you'll be on the shelf?" Amity asked, squeezing back.

"No, for I have a secret beau," Holly confided as the sleigh pulled up in front of the house. "Father doesn't approve of him, but I am in love with Lord Stanton."

The name meant nothing to Amity. "If Uncle Foster doesn't approve of him, why do you think he would give permission?"

"He won't, unless I can find a way to deter Mr. Poker-

Arse," Holly said with nonchalance. "I'm sorry, I know he was your dear friend. I oughn't speak that way."

"I shall never leave your side," Amity vowed. She gripped her wool cloak tight around her neck and let the footman hand her down from the sleigh. Holly's high spirits and penchant for intrigue ought to make for an entertaining Christmas holiday.

Chapter Two

Due to a renovation of the grand old pile of a house that had extended well past its projected completion date and would not be completed until spring, Finlay Weston had nowhere to stay at Christmas. Oh, there was his younger brother's neat home the next county over, or his sister's house in London, where she resided with her barrister husband and four small children, but young children gave him headaches. His mother had also taken up residence in Town. Logically, that was where he ought to spend the holiday.

Yet, there was Miss Holly Mayweather to consider. Her bright smile and sense of fashion made her an excellent prospective mistress of Weston Manor.

The coach struggled through the fresh snow and came around the bend, where the vista of Wells House spread before him as charming as a vista on a framed painting. Wells House glowed with welcoming lights in each window beneath its snowcap. Dusk had fallen hours ago. Somewhere behind the house, children might be out exploring the winter landscape—as he and his best friend Ellis Mayweather had done as children. Finlay felt his mouth pull into a half grin at the memory. Sledding. Tossing snowballs. Building forts.

A heartbeat later, he recalled the awful day when Ellis and his father had gone over a ledge in a carriage. They, two footmen and the horses had perished in the accident. Joy melted as easily as a snowflake on his cheek. The familiar seesaw of emotion was the primary reason he avoided spending much time here. Now that he was a grown man of twenty-six, however, it was time to make his mark on the crumbling country estate. It was time for him to take a wife.

Ideally, but not necessarily, one of means.

Lively, pretty Miss Mayweather would make an excellent companion. Finlay had approached her father to ask for her hand two weeks ago. Ever since, he could swear Miss Mayweather was avoiding him. When he showed up for a dinner, she laughed demurely and claimed her dance card was full. Which, in fairness, it generally was.

"Welcome, Mr. Weston," Mr. Mayweather intoned once the coach had halted and the footman released him from the confines of the carriage. "I trust you had an uneventful journey?"

"Indeed," Finlay replied. "No worse than could be expected."

Mayweather's jolly face tightened ever so subtly around the corners of his eyes and mouth.

"I meant, considering the heavy snowfall." Finlay continued hastily in an attempt to course-correct. "It was, as you say, an uneventful journey. I had time to anticipate with great pleasure the prospect of renewing my acquaintance with Miss Mayweather."

His phrasing was as stiff as an icicle, but Mayweather's features relaxed imperceptibly. "Of course. I expect Christmas to be a felicitous time to welcome you to the family." Mayweather raised his eyebrows suggestively. Finlay exhaled in relief. His childhood had been cut short at the age of fourteen when his father had perished unexpectedly. Ever since, he had strived to be as good a master of [ESTATE] as his father. "My staff will show you to your room. We shall gather in the parlor this evening for music and light dancing before supper."

Finlay's stomach gurgled with hunger. He hoped he could remember the complicated steps to a country reel, given how his brain had been commandeered by the grumbling of his empty belly. "Excellent, excellent."

Nothing felt excellent, however. Finlay bore it the way he had schooled himself to bear all discomforts and inconveniences of life—with the stiffest of stiff upper lips. Breakfast had been many hours ago, his stomach reminded him urgently. The journey had taken much longer than anticipated. Finn had expected to arrive in time for dinner, and here it was nearly suppertime.

His stomach plagued him to the point of irritability as Finlay dressed for dinner in buff trousers, a gold-embroidered ivory waistcoat and fresh cravat. Over this he added a deep blue jacket brushed to a high sheen of polished cobalt. Satisfied, he descended to join the gathering in the parlor. A tune from the pianoforte carried up the stairs, accompanied by a woman's lilting voice. He hesitated at the door to the gathering, ever feeling like an outsider. With his abrupt thrust into responsibility had come an unwarranted but crippling sense of inadequacy.

All he needed was a few moments alone with Miss Mayweather to ask whether she would have him for a husband. The sooner he negotiated the marriage settlement, the sooner he could go about posting banns. If the prospect of a wedding night with Miss Holly Mayweather left him cold, surely that was for the best. She might appreciate a husband who rarely darkened her door. Or, perhaps their marriage might kindle into flame upon closer acquaintance. For the moment, Finlay had selected his prospective bride the way one might evaluate a horse at auction. Teeth, hair, temperament, health.

No wonder the lady had avoided him.

"Our guest of honor," spoke Mr. Mayweather as Finlay entered the room. The lady's dulcet voice trailed off. The pianist hit a wrong note. Finn's empty belly rumbled loud enough to be heard by others

He cleared his throat and bowed to his future father-in-law. "I am honored to be a part of your celebration this Christmas."

"You remember my wife, Mrs. Mayweather," his host said, gesturing to a woman with rosy cheeks and blond curls similar to Holly's. Finlay did not remember her, a fact he blamed on the distraction of being unable to think of anything but food. Nonetheless he nodded over her gloved hand. Mayweather's wife beamed up at him. A good sign, Finn thought.

There was a whirlwind introduction to the other guests—men who heartily invited him to go shooting, married women who fluttered their hands at their breasts when he bowed, and youth in the first blooms of adolescence. Holly's sisters, brothers and cousins were too numerous for his sustenance-deprived brain to track. The one branch of the Mayweather clan missing this evening was Ellis's mother and sisters. A feeling worse than hunger pinched his heart.

"Would you care for mulled wine, Mr. Weston?" asked Mrs. Mayweather, offering a mug. "It's just the thing to chase away any lingering chill."

Finn accepted the vessel with a tight smile. The mere smell of spices and warm alcohol made him faintly sick. Not wanting to offend his hosts, he sipped the strong drink and regretted it immediately. "Thank you," he replied. "May I have a brief word with Miss Mayweather?"

"Which one? There are eight to choose from," the lady replied with a teasing twinkle in her eye.

Ha, ha. So clever. Finlay took another sip of the sticky, sweet wine. "I see where Holly gets her wit."

Mrs. Mayweather laughed as if he had paid her a great compliment. "Oh, very much. My eldest is my mirror image, many say."

If this was the case, Finlay had an excellent view of the kind of woman Holly would be in twenty years. He wasn't altogether certain he liked what he saw, in a romantic sense. Then again, if he were twenty years older, he might find the woman immensely attractive. Marriage was less about the heart and more about making a sensible match—and Holly was an eminently sensible choice of wife.

Mrs. Mayweather turned him toward the pianoforte. "Holly, do you remember Mr. Weston?"

The young woman perched elegantly on the edge of the piano bench wore a festive green gown trimmed with gold Vandyke points at the sleeve and hem. Her curls bobbed as she turned to face him with a haughty lift of her chin—quite a remarkable feat, considering how he loomed over her.

"Miss Mayweather," Finlay intoned, wishing he hadn't accepted the mug cooling in his hand. Nothing worse than cold mulled wine. "It is a pleasure to see you again."

Holly Mayweather barely suppressed an eye roll. Her lips stretched in a determined but distinctly unwelcoming smile that kept her even white teeth concealed.

I ought to have remained in my room for the evening. Finn had hoped to complete a transaction, not woo a reluctant bride.

"The pleasure is mine," Holly replied tightly. "I trust you remember my cousin, Miss Mayweather." With a smirk,

Holly turned to the lady leaning on the pianoforte with one arm.

Her name sprang to Finlay's lips unbidden. "Amity."

An electric shock jolted through his body. Finlay swallowed. Strands of dark hair that he'd last seen encrusted with twigs and bits of moss now dangled in glossy threads about her face. Amity Mayweather's snub nose had lost its freckles. Now it sloped delicately toward full lips and a stubbornly pointed chin. Above it, her green eyes danced with amusement.

His gaze skimmed downward, pulled by an inexorable gravity. My, Amity had grown tall, and round in all the— Shock sluiced through him. When had his best friend's little sister developed...breasts? The way her pert mounds filled the front of her white linen gown made his jaw tighten.

"Merry Christmas, Finn."

Finlay Weston braced against the onslaught of memories. Amity hoisting a stick as a sword above her head before knighting him with glancing blows to each shoulder. Her unabashed tackle about his waist took on an altogether inappropriate revision as he forced his gaze upward to meet hers. Hostility glittered in her eyes.

Amity had accurately guessed the course of his thoughts and did not welcome it one bit.

Too bad, that.

Chapter Three

Even as a growing boy, Amity's childhood playmate hadn't demolished a plate of ham the way Mr. Finlay Weston was doing at present. She exchanged glances with her cousin. Holly's plump mouth smoothed into a flat line as she poked her food with a silver fork, casting a doubtful eye at Finn when he accepted a second large helping. *Glutton*, Holly's expression silently accused.

Amity, meanwhile, concentrated on not spilling food on her new gown. To her immense relief, not one person had so much as raised an eyebrow at the sight of snowy-white linen embroidered with tiny red-and-green flowers. The lace at her sleeves and neckline had been carefully detached from the christening gown and sewn to the bodice of her new dress. It was to be removed and replaced upon her return. Her mother had pieced together the plaid accents from a section of the shawl moths had gotten to. Everything precious had gone into crafting this gown. Amity understood this was her mother's Christmas gift to her.

She also heard the unspoken plea: find a husband. Marry someone, anyone, who might relieve the pressure upon the family's finances. Amity thought of her sisters and mother sharing a simple roasted chicken and potatoes instead of this sumptuous feast. When she looked at things from a different angle, Finlay Weston's appetite was perfectly justified. Amity hadn't seen a feast like this in many years.

Finlay's dark hair, strong jaw and the sharp slope of his nose gave him a patrician air. He hadn't always been so serious. There remained no sign of the high-spirited boy she and Ellis had roamed the countryside playing pirates and highwaymen with. Finn had become a stranger in the years since she had last seen him.

Mr. Poker-Arse, Holly called him. Jealousy pooled up inside her like an underground spring eroding the foundation of an ill-situated house. Amity wished her marriage prospects included a wealthy, handsome man like Finn. Holly could afford to take suitors for granted. Amity couldn't. The uncharitable thought blew away the instant Mr. Mayweather raised a glass of wine. Sixteen adults were crowded around a table made to seat twelve. The children dined separately in the parlor. "I thank everyone who traveled through this historic snowfall to celebrate with us at Wells House this Christmas."

Amity sensed someone watching her from across the table and lifted her chin higher. It hurt to be a guest in her childhood home, but it was up to her whether she decided to hold on to that hurt or let it go. It was not her affair if Holly took her good fortune for granted—even if Amity couldn't stop thinking how if she had the interest of a man like Finn, she'd spend the evening smiling up at him no matter how ridiculous it made her appear.

An act that would last all of ten seconds. He knows the tart side of your tongue.

"A special welcome to our guest of honor, Mr. Weston. We

hope to soon have news to celebrate," Mayweather continued.

The gentleman whose name Amity hadn't quite caught banged his spoon against his wine glass. Others joined suit, and the room filled with the ringing endorsement of Holly's imminent betrothal. Her cousin's cheeks turned pink, then red, then scarlet. Finn cracked his first smile since the glimpsing a bread roll beside his dinner plate, as if Holly were like a delectable ham he couldn't wait to tuck into.

"What news might that be?" Amity asked innocently.

Spoons stopped their clanking as she placed her cup upon the crisp white tablecloth with strangely steady hands. Holly's blue eyes widened in gratitude. The table around her looked on in shock. It was unheard of, to press a couple into announcing themselves before they were ready. Finn frowned. Amity straightened her spine and sent him a haughty glare.

His full attention riveted upon her. Amity froze, her glass halfway to the table. The navy jacket made his eyes gleam unbearably bright blue. The sight stole her breath. Now, her heart raced. She clasped her hands in her lap to steady them.

"You shall know when the time is right," Finn responded with repressed consternation. *Mr. Poker-Arse, indeed*.

"I see." Amity replied in a voice that belied her trembling body. "I welcome your news, of course. I don't believe everyone present this evening does."

Silence descended. Mrs. Mayweather cast her a baleful look. Amity took a fortifying gulp of her punch. Holly's pink lips parted as if to speak, but Mrs. Mayweather clapped her hands and ordered the footmen to bring desserts before sound emerged. Amity closed her eyes. *What am I doing?*

Protecting her cousin from an unwanted marriage, that was what.

"Thank you." Holly clung to her elbow as the ladies

retreated to the parlor to gather the children and send them off to bed. "I was half afraid Weston would offer for me right there at the dinner table. Can you even imagine?"

"I'm sure he wouldn't embarrass you like that," Amity murmured. "Leave that to me."

"I was grateful for your intervention, even if Mother was not." Holly squeezed her arm. "You were magnificent, friend. My parents are pressing me to accept, as you have now seen." Her cousin's angelic features had pulled into a pout of dismay.

"Holly, you deserve better than a husband who regards you with respect but without passion. It would be a shame if you were to squander your freedom to choose a man you love." She forced a laugh, but it sounded bitter to her own ears. "Leave the joyless union to me."

"Don't say that, Amity. My parents have invited a few bachelor friends to celebrate the holiday. Perhaps one of them will appeal to you."

Across the room, Finlay regarded them with keen interest and arrogance. It shouldn't bother her that Holly scoffed at her old friend. Amity could hardly claim acquaintance with the stiff, arrogant man looking on like a hawk surveying a field for prey. Holly was a safe choice, a sensible one. Sensible men did not propose over the Christmas Eve feast. Despite her parents' intervention, Holly had always been safe from embarrassment, at least from Finlay.

Amity began to understand her mother's reluctance to remain on the premises of Wells House. If being displaced by her brother-in-law weren't bad enough, her aunt and uncle fancied themselves matchmakers. Amity forced as smile as Mrs. Mayweather coldly passed her a paper sheets of song lyrics. "Holly. If you will play the accompaniment."

Holly dutifully took her place at the pianoforte.

"Oh, dear. I haven't enough to go around." Mrs.

Mayweather held the last song sheet. "Mr. Lunt, do you mind sharing with Miss Amity?"

"Of course not," the man whose name Amity had been unable to recall at supper replied. She recognized a setup when she was strong-armed into one.

Pasting a smile on her face, Amity sidled up to the man her aunt had apparently suggested. He was not unhandsome. Mr. Lunt's ears stuck out and there appeared to be a thin spot at his crown, but he seemed nice enough. The man kept a respectful distance as he held the sheet low enough for her to see. Holly picked the opening bars to *While Shepherds Watched Their Flocks at Night.* Amity loved to sing and relished the opportunity to pour her heart into verse.

Mr. Lunt, however, could not carry a tune. Amity winced with each off-key note. Behind her, a resonant baritone reverberated up her spine. She edged away from Mr. Lunt and toward the delightful voice.

"Would you prefer to share my song sheet?" asked familiar voice, sotto voce. *Finn.*

Heat spread over Amity's chest and shoulders like a sudden rash. "I am quite fine, thank you," Amity replied with all the cold chill she could muster. It wasn't very much. Once the song had ended and Mrs. Mayweather had offered more mulled wine, Amity found herself standing close to Finn when they regrouped. Or, perhaps, he chose to stand near her. Either way, she detected the subtle scent of expensive soap and warm leather. Amity focused on the lyrics and tried to forget the tall man at her side.

"I don't comprehend your animosity toward me this evening, Amity." Finn spoke low as he flipped the page to *"The First Noel."*

Amity broke off mid-song and snorted. "For asking a simple question? My, you have become thin-skinned, Mr. Weston."

He regarded her speculatively from the corner of his eye. Heat flooded through her, pooling in her belly. Amity turned the page to their shared song sheet as her foolish heart raced. Surely, a man about to propose marriage ought to be single-minded in his interest toward his lady. Yet Finn barely glanced at Holly. Instead, he seemed fixated on her, lowly Amity, celebrating Christmas in her gown made from bed linens.

"It's almost as if you envy your cousin's imminent betrothal," replied Finn with studied casualness, his voice low enough that only she could hear his words. He balanced the hot wine in one hand and indicated she should turn the page again. Amity carefully breached the scant distance between them to flip it. The thrice-mended seam of her stained glove looked worse by candlelight than in the wan daylight of her bedroom at home. Embarrassed, Amity quickly dropped her hand. It knocked against a hard, solid object. Warm liquid splashed over her chest.

"Oh," she gasped.

Finn abandoned the drink on a nearby table to produce a handkerchief from his pocket. Awkwardly he began blotting at the red stains spreading across her bodice. "I had best let you take it from here," he said with genuine chagrin. "I seem to be making this worse, not better." Abruptly, he handed her the square of linen and turned away.

Amity was left staring down at her ruined dress in horror. Tears stung her eyelids. She refused to let them fall.

"Don't cry, dear," Mrs. Mayweather said gently. More gently than Amity deserved, considering her rudeness at dinner. "I've a maid who works wonders with stains. I'll bet my best bonnet she can get the wine out. Let's go and find her before it sets."

❄

The next morning, Finn awoke too late to attend Christmas church services, surely endearing him to his future mother-in-law. To his chagrin, he had also missed the children's gifts of oranges, nuts and small treasures. With his stomach full of spiced wine and too much food, he'd slept poorly. Twice he'd dreamed of a woman's plump and pert breasts, rolling them in his palm, teasing the dusky nipples into taut peaks. But when he'd looked up, it had been Amity's green eyes hooded with desire. After the first dream, Finn had buried his face in the pillow as shame had flooded through him at the memory of how he'd pawed Amity's breast with his handkerchief last night. When the hell had those developed? The last time he'd seen her, at Ellis's funeral, Amity's figure had still been distinctly girlish. He'd have remembered her chest, had it existed.

After the second time, Finn had awoken with a cockstand that had refused to subside until he'd taken matters in hand. After completion, he rolled over to sleep soundly at last.

Upon rising, Finlay took great care in choosing his garments. He had much to atone for if he wanted to secure Holly for his wife. And he did, very much. Her father's neighboring property, her fair countenance and natural vivaciousness made Holly an attractive bride. It ought to bother him that Holly didn't seem to enjoy his presence very much.

But what left him hollow was her cousin Amity's hostility. Until yesterday, on the rare occasions he'd thought of her it was as a hoyden playing stick swords and climbing trees with him and Ellis—sweet memories made too achingly painful to revisit often.

"Eating again, Mr. Weston?" Holly asked upon spotting him in the dining room breakfasting on cold sausages and rolls with bread and honey. She pulled her shawl up around her shoulders to shield her body from view—a gesture Finn might have found insulting had he been ogling her. As he hadn't been engaged in anything remotely of the sort, he chose to take the high road.

"My appetite is a testament to the excellence of your family's cook," he replied. Finn met her gaze and sat back in his chair. He wasn't about to be cowed by the woman he intended to marry. Needing breakfast and sleep were hardly grave offenses.

Amity appeared by Holly's shoulder, wrapped in a faded brown cloak. She paled at the sight of him. Finn experienced a similar jolt, which he covered by raising his fork to bite the end off of a sausage. "He's still growing into his ears," she smirked.

A streak of humiliation turned the sausage to sawdust in his mouth. Amity knew the precise soft spot to prod. Finn narrowed his eyes at her. If Amity wanted to be enemies, so be it. Finn did not want to fight her, though. Better if he could turn Amity into an ally in courting her cousin.

He set down his fork and rose to his full height. He straightened his forest-green waistcoat. "Miss Mayweather, I apologize for my clumsiness yesterday evening," he began. Amity's fine brows knit together in a scowl. "I trust your gown can be restored to its previous condition."

"We shall see if it can be salvaged," Amity replied tightly. Finn had the distinct impression that he had ruined more than a dress.

Chapter Four

How dare he.

Amity gazed around the other guests as she tried to put the unsettling contact with Finlay Weston out of her mind. The party included sixteen adults and nine children, who at the moment were outside sledding under the watchful eyes of the nursemaid and two footmen. Seven of the adults were unmarried.

Six geese a-laying. Five golden rings. Amity's mouth curved up at her unvoiced wit. She examined her prospects. Mr. Lunt, despite his unfortunate name, was her best bet. He owned property in Lancashire and was not an unattractive man if one overlooked his inability to carry a tune and trend toward baldness. As married names went, Amity Lunt did have a lumbering quality to it, however.

Her next best prospect was Mr. Gibbs, a short man with a prominent forehead and a lively humor that would have been more appealing if not for his laugh, a harsh donkey bray that made Amity wince each time she heard it. He held a decent living as a vicar. Marrying Mr. Gibbs wouldn't offer a significantly more comfortable life than what she had at Kearny, but

Amity knew how to scrimp and save. She could set aside a few shillings for her sisters.

Still. Amity Gibbs was an infelicitous name at best.

Her final option was Mr. Tillet. Quiet. Sober. Inscrutable. Amity didn't enjoy his presence enough to consider him for any reason beyond the pecuniary. He never laughed. He rarely smiled—and if he couldn't find a reason to smile at Christmas, when would he? Amity didn't have the heart to tie herself to such a dour man for the rest of eternity. She had promised her mother to try and find a husband, and Amity resolved to do so.

The only other unmarried man in the room was Mr. Finlay "Poker-Arse" Weston, and he was not an option. *How dare he.*

How dare Finn touch her breasts, even for the most innocuous reason? The memory of Finn's tall form at her back and his large hands brushing intimately against her body sent confusion churning through her. Amity didn't appreciate the way her skin heated with the slightest glimpse of Finn's broad back from across the room. She managed the problem by avoiding looking at him as much as possible, but she couldn't help sneaking occasional glances. Like Tillet, he was strong and quiet. Unlike Tillet, he still had a sense of wry humor and dry wit, honed to a fine point since childhood when what had passed for humor had been references to flatulence and poking one another with sticks. When he laughed, Finlay's chuckle rumbled through her like distant thunder, both warning and excitement. As for property, given the size of his annual income—a topic she ought to have paid more attention to as a young girl, before her world had fallen apart—Finlay Weston was well positioned to marry into the aristocracy.

Amity corrected the direction of her thoughts toward an innocuous plate of sugared plums. Finlay hoped to marry

Holly. Holly wanted to marry Lord Stanton, her exciting suitor in London.

What did *she* want? Amity had a sinking feeling that she knew, and he was already out of reach. Besides, she had promised Holly. One didn't renege on vows to a friend, even when she was starting to believe that perhaps that vow had been made in haste.

"Amity?" Holly looked at her expectantly. Lost in thought, Amity hadn't noticed her cousin's offer of a small parcel.

"Oh!" she said, recovering herself. Holly's bright blue eyes met hers. "Thank you." She had dreaded this moment. Amity had stitched a small square of linen left from the bedsheets with Holly's initials and a sprig of greenery beneath. She had traded her share of the egg money for wool thread, silk being out of the question. She had been too ashamed to give it to Holly once she had seen Holly's collection of fancy embroidered reticules perched on a shelf in her wardrobe. "I didn't realize there was to be a gift exchange. I left mine in your bedroom."

"No matter. Go on. Open it." Holly clapped her gloved hands. Her curls danced. In her white dress with green-and-gold accents, she looked like a giddy angel. She and Finlay made a handsome pair.

He leaned against the stone fireplace a few feet away and pretended not to observe their interaction. Amity swallowed. He had definitely grown into his ears. And his legs. Amity didn't care for the slippery, hollow ache that looking at him produced in her. Not when she could never have him. Finlay was destined for her cousin, and Amity's loyalty to Holly overrode whatever this temporary feeling for her old friend was called.

Infatuation, that was the term. Amity schooled herself not to pay Finlay no mind and lifted the heavy rectangular box lid with apprehension.

"A writing set," she breathed. A stack of thick paper as soft as her ruined dress lay in the tray. Proper goose quills and a sealed pot of ink lay in the tray, along with an unused block of sealing wax. Amity stroked the wood. It must have cost a month's worth of egg money. Two months, even. "Holly, I'm speechless."

"No more ridiculous scraps of paper, scatterbrain. I want proper letters from you all next year." Holly clapped her hands.

Amity bounced out of her chair to embrace her cousin. "Thank you," she whispered.

Amity's back warmed as if she were being watched. Near the mantle, Finn's dark gaze burned. Holly narrowed her eyes at him, and Amity broke contact.

Holly didn't want him.

Amity swallowed. Amity Weston had a nice ring to it.

How dare I?

❄

Finn found a welcome escape from Holly and Amity's sharp glances and sharper witticisms the next morning when he went out with the other men to hunt ducks in the pond down the hill from Wells House. The day after Christmas was the servants' holiday, leaving the family to fend for themselves and their guests with cold foodstuffs and hours of unstructured time. In the afternoon, the women would box up old garments and household wares to be distributed amongst the tenants of Wells House.

"I hear your property borders the Mayweathers," Mr. Gibbs said as a large plume of white fog emanated from his mouth. The shorter man struggled to keep up with Finn. Obligingly, Finn shortened his stride.

Snow overflowed the tops of his boots and melted against

his wool trousers. Wet trickled down the insides of his calves. In an hour, his feet would be bricks of ice. "It does," Finlay confirmed.

"I also hear you expect to secure a bride by the New Year," Gibbs panted.

"Word does seem to get around," Finn replied ruefully. There was no need for a hasty wedding, only that his two-week visit to the countryside presented an excellent opportunity to work out the details of Holly's marriage settlement with her father. He could return to London and see to his affairs without the process dragging on past Twelfth Night. But first, he needed to secure the lady's agreement. It was lowering to find that this was proving to be the most difficult aspect to the process. Finlay had rarely needed to make an effort to attract a lady's interest. His fortune did that for him.

"I understand it's Miss Mayweather who has captured your interest," puffed Gibbs. "You'll make a handsome couple."

"Mr. Gibbs, is there a point to your questions?" Finn asked in exasperation. Ahead, the rest of the men trudged along through the snowpack. Mayweather led the way, his great wool-clad form lumbering bear-like through the drifts.

"I wish to know whether you have any claim upon Miss Amity Mayweather," Gibbs replied bluntly.

A hot spike of *no* struck Finn's heart. "None at all," he replied gruffly.

"I ask," Gibbs panted, "because it seems you have a prior acquaintance with her. I don't wish to intrude where my suit is not welcome."

"I imagine your suit would be as welcome as any other man's," Finn offered, feeling parsimonious. "Although her younger sister's temperament is more aligned with your calling."

Gibbs laughed. The harsh sound startled a duck, which

took wing. Mr. Mayweather, who had moved into position behind a stand of bushes while they chatted, fired. "Good shot, old chap," Gibbs called out. The wounded bird fluttered to earth. Red blood stained the crisp snow. A tawny spaniel bounded through the drifts at the edge of the pond to retrieve is body. "About Miss Mayweather's sister. You were saying?"

"Miss Mary Anne Mayweather is devoted to religious study," was all Finn said. But was it still true? Amity had never been much given to religion. She observed the niceties, of course, but it was Mary Anne who had memorized the Bible. Finn wondered whether the intervening years had softened her religious leanings. He ought to pay a visit to the family.

"Considering that I wear my faith lightly," Gibbs replied, setting the stock of his gun against his shoulder and peering down the barrel, "I believe Miss Amity Mayweather's company will suit me better."

"You have excellent instincts," Finlay replied as evenly as he could manage. Would that Finlay had demonstrated the same savvy. He had no claim on his old friend's affections. If anything, he ought to be facilitating Amity's suitor, not attempting to direct his attentions elsewhere. Gibbs would make Amity a fine husband, Finlay reminded himself as he spied a winged black dot on the edge of the frozen pond.

Yet there was no denying the fact that he wanted Amity far more than he did her cousin. Finn's desire could not be attributed solely to wayward dreams of her unexpected breasts, either. For all of Holly's beauty, there were moments when her high spirits bordered on flightiness. At twenty-two years old, and after three seasons in London, Holly had acquired a polished sheen of expensive gowns and pricey shawls but no apparent interest in acquiring a husband to provide such luxuries. If only Finn had considered this before approaching Holly's father. Now, however, there was no backing out.

Fortunately for the ducks, his aim was off when he fired.

"There's a fat little partridge in the bush just there." Gibbs pointed with one gloved hand. He set about reloading. "I'll bet you can't knock it out of the tree."

Finlay squinted in the bright winter light until a small oval-shaped bird took form on one forlorn branch. It looked so cozy in its hiding spot, feathers fluffed, beady eyes warily scanning the pond for the source of all this racket. He readied his gun and aimed. At the last second, Mayweather's spaniel bounded through the nearby bushes. Finlay fired. The indignant partridge bolted out of range. Finlay wished it Godspeed.

"Ach, stupid beast. Mayweather ought to have trained his dog better," Gibbs grumbled with ill temper. Their man-to-man conversation was over. The other man floundered off through knee-deep snow to find the other men. Finn patted the dog's head until Mayweather whistled, and the animal bounded happily away. His toes had gone numb, so when Mayweather ordered the men back to the house, he was content to leave the flock in peace as befit the spirit of the season. Besides, any longer out here and he was liable to take aim at the next man who asked him about Amity—and that was not a comfortable thought at all.

❄

"Incoming!"

The shout came one second before the plop of wet snow hit Finlay's cheek. It didn't hurt, exactly. Cold bit his into his skin and startled him out of his thoughts. He ducked the next one and scooped up a palmful of wet snow. Packing into a tight ball wasn't easy with his firearm lodged in the crook of his arm, but he managed to form a ball and lob it back at the female form who'd hit him in the face. His aim was better with frozen water than with a firearm this morning. He knocked her hat off her head. Blond hair tumbled around her shoulders. Holly shrieked.

"I give as good as I get!" Finlay called out. Fuming, Holly recovered her hat and glared. What could have been an exhilarating exchange wilted into uneasy disappointment. Nearby, the children had built a snow fort and amassed quite a stockpile of ammunition. Two heads took turns popping up to bombard him with badly aimed snowballs. The rest of the children attacked the other men. The surprise attack must have been in the works all morning. Mr. Mayweather had dropped his gun unceremoniously into the snow to retaliate with enthusiasm. Only Tillet held back. *Sod him*, Finn thought as he discarded his unloaded weapon and charged at the children's fort with a battle cry. The children yelled and pelted him with snow until he crashed over the edge of their monument into a pile of snowballs and wet wool.

"Oof, get off me, Finlay!" an outraged woman yelped, breathless.

He'd landed crossways over Amity's midsection. A grin took over his face. It figured that Amity would be leading the mischief. She scowled and gave him a shove. When Finn didn't move, she bared her teeth and began to kick her way out from under him. The children grabbed at his clothing in an attempt to pull him away. Finlay's body responded to Amity's warm, wiggling form. He pushed himself to his feet before he could embarrass himself. Amity rolled over and bounced up. Her dark hair stuck in damp strands to her cheek. Her green eyes blazed with outrage…and something more. Memories of their play as children cartwheeled through his mind, happy recollections, tinged with a sharp sting of sadness as Ellis's ghost intruded between them. Once, they had been close.

White steam stained the air between them. They weren't children anymore.

Finn couldn't ignore how much he wanted to kiss her. Amity gazed up at him, her glare softening. Her lips parted as if in welcome. Behind them came a harsh bark of adult anger, followed by a child's wail.

"Mr. Weston!" Holly called out. "I am about to lose my fingers and toes to frostbite, and Adam is crying. Don't just stand there. Help us gather the children."

The spell broke. Amit's expression hardened into mutiny as she marched over to her cousin to help her with the crying boy. A slimy streak beneath his red nose mixed unappealingly with the child's tears. Holly's curls bounced around her shoulders in a tangle as she gathered him into her arms. She was the very picture of maternal concern. Amity…

Was nothing but an old friend for whom he had developed uncomfortable, inconvenient feelings. It was nothing more than the effects of shared memories, Finlay told himself. Yet, it was Amity's hips churning beneath her serviceable cloak that pulled at him. He retrieved his rifle and trudged back to the house.

"Did you hurt the boy?" Finlay demanded of Gibbs.

"The brat deserved it," Gibbs huffed. "God made children to obey, not to assault their betters with snowballs."

Finlay decided instantly there was one man who wouldn't be marrying Amity—not if he had anything to say about it.

Chapter Five

"Don't let him kiss me," Holly pleaded, shoving Amity roughly into place beneath the mistletoe.

"I don't think he wants to," Amity whispered back, exasperated. The past forty-eight hours had made her question whether her cousin's taste in gentlemen were quite on point. Would a poker-arse leap into the middle of a child's snowball fight?

No. Nor would a poker-arse leap over the wall of a fort and crush a woman breathless.

Finlay stood a few feet away, his back to them. Amity planted herself in the door frame as the guests prepared to play a post-tea game of Blind Man's Bluff. Mrs. Mayweather stood in the middle of the parlor, explaining the rules to the younger children. Mr. Gibbs and Mr. Mayweather had retired to the library, to Amity's great relief, leaving the rest of the family to entertain themselves. She hoped Mr. Gibbs was getting the dressing-down he deserved after having pushed an eight-year-old face-first into a snowbank. A grown man ought to be able to take a snowball from a child without losing his temper, even if it had hit him directly in the face.

Amity had been too busy locking gazes with Finn to see it happen, much to her shame.

Her pulse pounded at how quickly memories of what had been had turned to thoughts of what might blossom between them if it weren't for Holly.

What could never be. One thing was clear after today, though. Finlay Weston was anything but Mr. Poker-Arse. His natural thoughtfulness may have hardened into reserve, but what else ought she to expect from a man who had shouldered so much responsibility at such a young age?

Finlay might not be as exciting a beau as Holly had wished for, but upon closer acquaintance, Amity found little fault and much to admire. Idly, she imagined tracing the broad span of his shoulders as her gaze followed the V of his back downward to the two buttons at his waist. The cut of his jacket concealed the precise shape of his buttocks, but Amity could conjure a guess as to their shape if it matched the rest of him. She had years of stored-up longing to inform her conjecture, after all. The worst part of having fallen into poverty was that she and her sisters still yearned for men with genteel manners who wore well-cut clothing. Well, she did, anyway. Letty and Charity were less particular. They had been so young when the family had fallen on hard times that they were less enamored of the upper class. Amity, though, keenly felt the difference.

Kearny has many good, hardworking men, she reminded herself sternly. There were also plenty of gentlemen with less than admirable—

"Are you ready for a kiss, Miss Mayweather?" asked Mr. Lunt.

A faint flush spread over his cheekbones. Amity glanced around, then up at the green sprig with white berries suspended upon a red ribbon directly above her head. "No, in truth I had forgotten about the—" She stiffened as Lunt bent to silence her with a kiss directly on the mouth.

She pursed her lips against the intrusion. It was not her first shy peck beneath the mistletoe—the stuff grew on every blackthorn bush, and even the destitute branch of the Mayweather family could afford greenery at Christmastime—but it was the first time a man had attempted to insert his tongue in her mouth. What a disgusting practice, and for him to do it in front of the entire family was humiliating. Her heart raced as Amity tried to pull away, but Lunt wasn't done. He wrapped his arm around her waist and anchored her against his chest. Amity pushed futilely against Lunt's shoulder.

"That's quite enough," a male voice warned.

Lunt released her. Amity stumbled backward. Her lips felt coated with slime. She dared not wipe away for fear of offending him. When she found Holly, her cousin's bright blue eyes were clouded with uncertainty. A strong arm gently caught Amity about the shoulders. Reassuring. Steadying.

Finn.

Lunt had reached up to pluck white berries from the branch of mistletoe. He rolled the little white beads in his palm. Nervous droplets beaded on his forehead.

"Well, Mr. Lunt, that was delivered with admirable enthusiasm. How would you like to be our first blind man this evening?" Mrs. Mayweather's sister, Holly's aunt through her mother's side, arrived with a tray laden with festive biscuits and bonbons.

Holly turned away as though she was embarrassed of Amity. Everything had happened in the blink of an eye as Amity stood rooted to the floor in shock and shame.

"I hope we have many children, Miss Mayweather," Lunt said quickly. He grabbed her hand and poured the little white berries into her palm. "If I may have the first dance with you this evening."

"Of course," Amity replied woodenly. What else was she supposed to say?

Lunt was a gentleman, ostensibly. She had, after all, been standing under the mistletoe at Christmas. Yet kisses were supposed to be chaste and gentle, not sweaty public attacks upon her person. Amity stared down at the white berries in her palm and felt the blood drain from her face. *I hope we have many children.*

"Did he say the words I think I heard?" Amity muttered to Finn's tall, solid presence. She couldn't bring herself to meet his gaze.

"Yes," Finn replied quietly. Her embarrassment ballooned inside her chest.

No, the worst part was that Finn had witnessed her brief defilement. Had Holly set her up, or had her cousin genuinely wanted to avoid kissing Finlay? And if so, why?

It had been only a kiss, yet Amity felt violated. The worst part was that Holly wouldn't look at her now, as though Lunt's unwanted embrace had tainted Amity. Holly popped a confectionery into her mouth as her attention slid past Amity. Lunt appeared oddly satisfied with himself, his chest puffed as he dangled a thick white scarf from his fingers, ready to be the Blind Man.

"I don't know if anyone has said it explicitly," Finlay said with a grimace, "but you ought to know the reason for the presence of three bachelors this Christmas is that you are said to be seeking a husband. Your uncle believes it is time for you to marry. Mr. Lunt, Mr. Gibbs and Mr. Tillet are his selections for your delectation."

"None. I refuse all of them," Amity said with all the fervor she didn't know how to conceal. "Finn, my uncle listens to you. Will you ask him to call them off?"

"I cannot." They were standing together now beneath the kissing bower, Finlay leaning one arm against the woodwork as if to protect her. "But I can try to prevent that from happening again. I don't like what Lunt did to you just now. Undoubtedly, he will find your reticence a sign of modesty and not disinterest. He's a grown man and ought to know the difference, yet…" he trailed off. "I can't call the others off from their pursuit."

"Not even for an old…friend?" Amity asked, peering up at him through the fringe of her hair. His image swam, and Amity realized with horror that she was on the verge of tears.

"I'll do what I can to protect you, Amity," he whispered, straightening as the players gathered in a circle. Holly still avoided her, to Amity's mortification. "Though I confess my feelings for you are…" Finlay broke off. He shook his head.

"Are what?" Amity demanded.

Finn shook his head.

"You can't stop there," she protested, but he turned his back on her to join the game. A muscle in his jaw worked. Amity narrowed her gaze at him and, in a childish fit of frustration, tossed a white berry at his back. It bounced off and fell to the carpet to be squished underfoot. She deposited the remaining fruit on a side table and edged back into the festivities, eager to shake the sense that Lunt's kiss had made her a pariah. She kept a watchful eye on Lunt. The odious man wore a smug expression when he finally caught the youngest girl, who was seventeen and old enough to stay up with the adults.

Amity edged her way into the parlor enough to see that he was utterly correct with the girl. He handed over the blindfold and stepped adroitly out of the way as the girl barreled around the room, seeking a new victim. He sidled nervously over to Amity. "I didn't mean to embarrass you."

"It's all right." Amity swallowed. The best gift she could

bring to her mother this holiday season was an offer of marriage. Lunt, Gibbs and Tillet were her only chances of obtaining a proposal. Yet all she could think of was how badly she wished that kiss had come from Finlay, instead.

There were five days until the New Year, with toasts to health and prosperity. Five days more until the Twelfth Night ball—and after that, she could return home. Unless she decided to reach for one of the men her uncle had selected for her.

Again, her gaze strayed to Finn. Holly claimed not to want him.

What if Amity did?

❋

"You saved my life this evening," Holly declared with a shudder as she swept a brush through her gleaming locks in the privacy of her bedroom.

"It was no great sacrifice," Amity mumbled. She tucked her wrapper around her legs. What a joy to have enough candlelight to read into the evening. She paused and placed a ribbon between the pages of her book, borrowed from the Mayweather's generously appointed library. She remembered this book, a bawdy romance her mother had declared inappropriate for a girl her age when Amity had first discovered it. Reading the story again was like visiting an old friend. "Holly, why don't you want to marry Finlay?"

Holly set her brush aside. "It's not his person I object to. It's that he spoke to Father without coming to an understanding with me first. I have already given my heart to Lord Stanton. It's only a matter of time before he proposes, I swear."

"Aren't you afraid that marriage to an aristocrat is a stretch, even for you? Is he a baron or a viscount?"

"I can't believe you don't know." Holly sigh, irritated. "Don't all young ladies memorize *Debrett's?*"

No, some of us are too busy tending chickens and pulling weeds to put food on the table. Not that Amity's mother would ever dream of asking the rest of the Mayweather family for monetary assistance. Amity wished her mother had been more forthcoming about the arrangements than her unspoken implication that Amity was to find a suitor during this visit. "I haven't had any reason to do so," she replied mildly. With her newfound comprehension of the Mayweather's matchmaking machinations, Holly's embarrassed response after Lunt's kiss made sense. Holly must have been ashamed of her parents putting Amity in an awkward position.

But then, why wouldn't she say so out loud? Amity swallowed her disappointment.

"Lord Stanton is an earl," Holly informed her haughtily. She set her hairbrush down on the dresser and checked her appearance in the mirror above it. "Father doesn't approve. I told him I wanted to return to London in the spring and why. He told Mum, and the next I knew, Mr. Weston was to join us for Christmas. She is so excited about having Mr. Weston for a son-in-law. I feel as if everyone has conspired to marry me off without ever consulting me on the subject."

"A perfectly fair response," Amity replied slowly. "In fact, I suspect the same thing has happened to me. Finn says your father invited Mr. Lunt, Mr. Gibbs and Mr. Tillet specifically to court me. Do you know anything about this?"

Holly's gaze slid guiltily away from hers. "Mother thinks you and your sisters are too poor to find proper husbands. Once I asked to invite you for the holidays, they wanted to help. But subtlety isn't their strong suit."

"You might've at least warned me," Amity rebuked mildly. "It's not the intent that bothers me. It's the sneakiness of it." The Mayweathers' underlying assumption that she was incapable of finding a husband burned. Worse, they hadn't evaluated their chosen prospective husbands with any knowledge of the kind of man she might find attractive.

Finn.

"Yes, well, it seemed as if you might welcome attentions from at least one of the men," Holly huffed. "I thought it might go more naturally if you met them without pressure."

Clearly, Holly had inherited her parents' propensity to scheme. "Considering how you don't wish to marry Mr. Poker-Arse—"

Holly interrupted her with a laugh. "I daresay Tillet has usurped Mr. Weston's title. Have you ever met such a dreary man?"

"No." Amity chuckled. She did not wish to fight with her cousin. She abandoned her book and came to the bed she was sharing with Holly. "But since you don't want Finlay to ask for your hand…"

"I never said that," Holly replied quickly.

"Yes, you did." Amity remembered their conversation in the sleigh distinctly. "You begged me not to leave your side so Finn wouldn't have a chance to propose. You wanted to go back to London and your Lord Stanton, remember?"

Her cousin rolled onto her side and took the bulk of the coverlet with her. "Stop hogging the warm spot. My feet are freezing," she complained, kicking at Amity's stockinged feet.

"Then give me half the blanket," Amity replied. Her frustration ran deeper than a squabble over a down comforter and the heat from a pan of coals. The iciness between them was more than temperature. It had frozen hard into a sheet of resentment.

"I have decided I rather like Mr. Weston. I believe I shall permit him to catch me beneath the mistletoe next time," Holly huffed. "I still don't wish to marry him, but Mum is right. I could do worse for a husband. I ought to at least allow him to court me for a few days, just in case Lord Stanton doesn't make an offer after all."

"Then I don't need to provide you with constant companionship," Amity replied with a bitterness she couldn't quite conceal.

"That's right."

"I may socialize with whomever I choose, then?"

"Certainly. Although I doubt you'll have much opportunity for that. Mr. Gibbs asked Papa for permission to ask for your hand this evening. That's what they were doing in the library while you were kissing Mr. Lunt."

Amity sucked in a breath. *That wasn't how it happened.* "I'd rather it had been Finn who'd kissed me. At least I would have enjoyed it."

Holly stiffened. Amity knew immediately she had said exactly the wrong thing at precisely the wrong moment. Yet, having dug the first scoop for her grave, she found it impossible to put the shovel down.

"You wouldn't dare," her cousin replied.

"Why not? You don't want him."

Holly threw back the coverlet and sat up. "That is untrue. Apologize, or find somewhere else to sleep."

"Holly, it's ten o'clock at night. I refuse to go wandering about in my wrapper with three different men staying in the house who have designs on me." Amity took advantage of Holly's indignation to pull the blanket more firmly around her body. Much warmer.

"Out," her cousin commanded, pointing to the door.

"Don't be such a child," Amity replied as she snuggled deeper into the soft bed. "Finn is a person, not a toy to fight over. We shall handle this like grown women and do a far better job of it than letting your parents make our decisions for us." Holly's furious expression softened, so Amity continued. "We should both indicate to Finn that we welcome his advances and let the man choose between us."

Holly tossed her head. "Fine. I have no doubt he will choose me."

The mattress dipped and the bedclothes rustled as Holly climbed back into the warm spot she had just vacated. Amity could guess precisely what her cousin was thinking. Holly possessed ample beauty and a substantial dowry. Amity had neither. There was no possible way Finn would choose her over Holly. Yet the embarrassment would be worth it in the end, for at least it would let her put the formidable Finlay Weston between Lunt, Gibbs, and Tillet.

She *was* jealous. Her cousin regarded Finlay as a convenient backstop for a more ambitious match that might not work out, whereas Amity...

Loved him.

She always had. For so many years, she had chosen to remember Finlay Weston as a beanpole boy with a shy smile, ears like jug handles, and a level head that tempered the worst of Ellis's extravagant imaginings. Along with his ears, Finlay had grown into a gentleman of reserved kindness and gentle humor. Precisely the sort of man she could imagine teasing and sharing stories with for years to come. Yet, regardless of her wishes, she must marry. At least now that she knew the score, Amity could evaluate the men before she accepted one of them for her husband. What harm was there in including Finlay in their little competition? Amity just hoped she didn't lose her cousin's friendship in the process.

Chapter Six

The next morning marked a confounding shift in Holly's attitude toward Finlay. There were no snide comments about his appetite, which had returned to normal. No one-word replies when he inquired about how well she had slept. In fact, Holly had taken him off guard with a brightly delivered, "Good morning, Mr. Weston." Beside her, Amity watched and listened without attempting to intervene in her cousin's incessant stream of chatter.

Curious.

The minute he had resolved to speak with Holly's father about releasing him from proposing to Holly, the lady in question developed a keen interest in him. He was caught in a net of his own making woven from conflicting strands of honor and desire. Finlay could hardly spurn the woman he'd planned to marry, in her own home, at Christmas. Only a cad would humiliate her so.

Fresh snow had fallen in the night, and the crowded house was beginning to feel claustrophobic. He was not alone in wanting a bit of fresh air, for Holly leaped at his proposal of a post-breakfast sleigh ride before he could even finish speaking.

"I would be delighted to accompany you." She beamed.

Finlay's breakfast suddenly tasted off. This was the ideal opportunity to ask her to marry him. Yet even if Amity had not stolen his heart beneath snow and mistletoe, Holly's overnight pivot from cold disdain to enthusiasm left him suspicious of her motives. Her radiant smile sharpened into a smirk. Finn followed the direction of her narrow gaze and found…

Amity. She poked at her eggs, flanked by Gibbs and Lunt. Tillet sat next to Mrs. Mayweather, chatting agreeably about the clear weather.

"Perhaps Amity would like to join us?" he asked.

Mrs. Mayweather stopped speaking midsentence to gape at him. Her mouth closed in a flat line that said clearly, *What are you doing?*

Spoiling the perfect opportunity to achieve his goals, that was what. Intentionally, at that.

"Mr. Tillet, would you care to accompany my niece?" Mrs. Mayweather asked sweetly.

Check and mate. Mrs. Mayweather was not going to let him worm out of doing the honorable thing toward her daughter—not easily.

"Certainly," Tillet replied. Finn was startled at the sound of his resonant bass voice. Yet it conveyed no enthusiasm, flat in affect and tone. Gibbs and Lunt spoke at Amity from either side, paying little attention to their hostess's machinations until the matter was settled, too late for them to join.

"Excellent. I shall have the horses readied after breakfast." Mr. Mayweather replied, seemingly pleased with the arrangement. More so than Finn could claim to be—but at least Amity would be close by, where he could protect her from further assaults upon her person.

They set out a half hour later with Tillet in the front seat, next to the driver, and Finn in the rear seat between two women whom had been fast friends as recently as yesterday. Now they ignored one another as studiously as the opposite faces of a Janus statue. Once they were gliding over the snow, however, Holly warmed up instantly—to Finlay, at any rate.

Her hand beneath the blanket went places it oughtn't. Up his thigh, close to his nether regions. Whereas two days ago he might have welcomed her forwardness, Finn had the distinct sense that now it was borne out of peeved aggrievance instead of affection. He captured her small hand in his and removed it from his person. A moment later it was back, though she kept her hand lower on his knee.

"I find the Christmas holiday most invigorating, don't you?" Tillet asked, turning in his seat to speak generally to all three of them, most directly to Amity.

"Indeed," she replied, properly reticent.

Before Amity could say anything further, Holly jumped in. "I simply love the candles and the gift-giving and the rosemary and mistletoe, and the carols. Best of all, though, is being together with family." Holly batted her eyes at him. Finn couldn't recall ever having been simpered at with this degree of enthusiasm by anyone, much less Holly Mayweather. "Especially the singing," she continued when he didn't respond. "You have such a wonderful voice, Mr. Weston."

Finlay Weston knew blarney when he heard it. Yesterday, Holly had barely been able to tolerate his presence. Today, she was all smiles and inappropriately intimate touches. The abrupt turnabout gave him the distinct sense that she couldn't stand the idea of his attraction to her cousin. Amity, by contrast, sat tight-lipped and coiled like a spring beside him.

"Not so wonderful as Mr. Tillet's," Finn said. He could play along with Holly, but Amity's silence worried him.

"You are as kind as you are misguided," replied Tillet. Despite his brooding countenance, Tillet wasn't a bad match for Amity. Finlay stifled a grimace at the thought.

"Sing us a song." Holly clapped. "Both of you, together."

Oh, very well. If he couldn't indulge with a song for the new year, what use were winter holidays?

"I must demur, Miss Mayweather. My throat has been sore these past few days. I don't wish to tax my voice." Tillet replied in a voice that sounded perfectly fine to Finlay's ears.

"Is that why you've been so quiet?" Holly asked.

Beside him, Amity stiffened at her cousin's rudeness. "Holly. Please. What might be an acceptable flirtation in London is the height of inconsideration here in the countryside," Amity chided her gently.

"I beg your pardon?" Holly demanded with affront. Finn began to feel like a tennis ball bouncing between the arguing women. Amity was right. Holly's lighthearted and thoughtless banter served her well in London, but in the countryside, here barbs were too pointed to be kind. Finn wondered how he had failed to see it before. That spoke poorly of his judgment. He too had been blinded by expectations for marriage. He had taken Holly's banter personally. Now, he knew that Holly was a flirt.

"You needn't badger Mr. Tillet about his reticence, cousin. In fact," Amity declared with narrowed eyes, "you might consider exercising some yourself."

"Ladies, as much as I appreciate your active discussion, it makes me blush to be the subject of such controversy. Please, for my sake, be friends," Tillet asked. Finn's estimation of the older man rose.

Holly pouted and took the excuse to wiggle her way

beneath his arm. Finn stiffened. He shifted away, but Holly leaned closer against him until there was a six-inch gap between her and the right wall of the sleigh. From his left, he had moved so close against Amity that he belatedly realized he might be crushing the breath out of her. Awareness coursed through him as he shifted to give her more space. This had the unfortunate effect of increasing his contact with Holly. Carefully, he eased his arm out from between them and stretched it across her shoulders. Amity, a few inches taller than her cousin, nestled perfectly against him.

"Well, look at this." Tillet chuckled. "A cozy winter scene if there ever was one."

They glided over the snow. Holly continued to burrow inappropriately against his side. She strokes his knee, which made Finlay stiffen and jerk his leg away. Was she under the mistaken impression that accosting his person was the way to win his heart? The way she petted him and curled like a kitten against him didn't make Finlay want her more. It made him feel like an object used for retaliation in her argument with Amity.

Amity studiously ignored her cousin. She remained stiff beside him while the wintry scene whisked by. The sleigh whisked up to the portcullis of Wells House. A few stray snowflakes danced in the air as Finlay handed down Holly. Amity had accepted Tillet's assistance. They stood huddled beneath the shelter. Snow dotted Amity's dark eyelashes like tiny diamonds. Envy clutched his innards.

"I regret that I must depart this afternoon," Tillet said, looking indeed contrite. "I wish that I had been so fortunate to meet such a lovely young lady before committing myself elsewhere," he said, raising Amity's gloved hand to brush a kiss over the back. "Alas, I am recently engaged. I wish you great success in finding your own match, Miss Mayweather. The other Miss Mayweather too."

Tillet glanced over at Finlay and winked. A shock ran through his body. Was their awkward little trio's dynamic so obvious?

"Oh." Amity said, taken aback. "I wish you a quick recovery from your croup and a happy nuptial." Was Finlay imagining it, or did she look crestfallen?

Amity could not have been entertaining him as a suitor. Finlay's fists clenched at his sides. He flexed them open and closed as though he might wrap them around Tillet's neck.

"Do come and visit us again soon," Holly interjected, grabbing Tillet by both hands. "I hope to have similarly happy news to report upon our next meeting." She cast a sidelong simper at Finn. He swallowed. Amity's gaze dropped to her feet. How disappointing it must feel to be rejected.

"As do I," Finn said as he bowed to Tillet. But it was not the shorter blonde beside him who blushed. Amity's cheeks turned pink from more than the cold. Beside him, Holly stamped her foot, breaking the spell.

"I must go inside before I lose my toes to frostbite. Come, Amity." Holly took her cousin by the arm and marched her into the house, where the yule log burned low and bright.

"Miss Holly is a fine lady," Tillet offered once the women had gone inside and the driver had taken the horses around back to be unhitched.

"She is," Finn said repressively.

"She would make a fine wife," Tillet added. "As would Miss Amity."

"You speak out of turn," Finlay declared with heat in his voice.

Tillet responded with a knowing smile. "The Mayweathers are good people, but they believe too firmly in their infallible judgment. Had I known Mr. Mayweather believed I might propose to Amity, I would have remained in my bachelor's quarters in London for the holiday. I came here in hopes to conclude a small matter of business unrelated to marriage." Tillet smiled ruefully. "I find I cannot get any time with Mayweather, as it seems our host has grandiose ambitions to play matchmaker this season."

Finlay grimaced, for he had dived headfirst into the drama the way he had done with Ellis and Amity when they'd been children jumping into the river that marked the border between the Mayweather and Weston estates.

"A bit of romance of holidays can be a lovely thing," Tillet observed.

"'Tis not a bad thing to want, when all the players are aware and informed," grumbled Finlay.

Tillet sent him a speaking glance. "I must be going. It looks as though you have a dilemma to sort out. I wish you the best of luck with it." Tillet tipped his hat and left Finlay to kick at the snow, wondering how to untangle this mess. A certain base part of him was flattered at the prospect of two pretty ladies going to war over his affections—which might be enticing if his body was not similarly at war with his mind. Men's heads were placed above their hearts, and Finlay Weston was not about to make the mistake of reversing the natural hierarchy that placed reason above affection.

※

W*hen can I go home?* Amity wondered miserably. Across the room, Holly engaged everyone around her in conversation about nothing and everything. Every few seconds, her eyes darted to Finn as if to say, *can't you see how much everyone likes me?*

Finlay, to his credit, mostly ignored her cousin's increasingly obvious bids for attention. Amity had never been embarrassed of Holly until this evening. But then, she had only known her cousin from letters ever since she'd had her first season. Holly had changed, and not for the better.

Amity eyed Mr. Gibbs warily. Every few minutes, he cast her a longing glance. Each time, it sent a shiver of disgust through her body. She had avoided the mistletoe hanging above the parlor doorway, going out of her way to exit through the dining room to keep from passing beneath it. Amity shuddered every time she recalled the punishment of his kiss. This morning, Mr. Tillet had shot to the top of the list of men from whom Amity might consider accepting a proposal, and he had departed for London immediately after dinner.

Which was not altogether a disaster, considering the maids had arranged for her to take his room. The prospect of sharing a bed with her cousin as she gloated about Finlay had worried Amity all day.

"You look displeased."

Amity started. Finn's cool voice at her side had the opposite effect of Gibbs' unfeigned interest. Her stomach clenched. She replied under her breath. "I apologize for Holly's behavior—"

"Don't," Finlay replied, cutting her off. "Her behavior her own responsibility. Not yours. All she has done is flirt with an excess of enthusiasm. Any young woman might be excused—"

"After giving you the cold shoulder for days," she responded with heat. "It speaks to an unbecoming inconstancy. I fear my cousin has been spoiled by her excessive time in London. Three seasons, going on four…"

Amity trailed off as she recognized her own jealousy speaking. She clapped one gloved hand over her mouth to stop words she would regret from spilling out.

Finlay gently urged her around the corner from the parlor, where the Mayweathers and their guests had gathered around the still-burning yule log for a game of charades. They could speak privately yet be visible and therefore appropriate. "Your cousin's indiscretions are far more forgivable than what Lunt did to you. Are you all right?"

Amity wasn't, and now that she was friendless in a house full of people who had conspired in secret to marry her off without consulting her on the subject, she needed a friend more than ever. Shame at her initial spitefulness toward her old friend washed over Amity. "I wish my first kiss hadn't been so unwelcome," she mumbled.

"Your first kiss?" Finn echoed in surprise.

Amity's face burned. She might as well have said, *we are too poor for me to attract gentleman callers*. How embarrassing it was to reveal her family's circumstances. "Yes," she confirmed. They had edged away from the doorway, out of sight from the game taking place.

"Then we ought to make sure your second kiss makes up for the awfulness of your first."

Amity's gaze met his. Heat streaked down her midsection.

"With your permission?"

She nodded once. Finlay tilted her chin up, and his mouth closed over hers. Warm. Gentle. Perfect.

Amity sighed. Finn's palm found her waist. His thumb skimmed her ribcage in an echo of the many times he had held her down and tickled her until she'd breathlessly fought free. When was the last time she had felt that carefree? A lifetime ago…and now, here in his arms. Finn nipped the plump center of her lower lip. She gasped. Finn teased her mouth until she parted, giving pleasure, waiting at each intrusion for her to indicate she welcomed his embrace. She opened to him in welcome. Finn anchored his arm around her waist and teased her tongue with his. His free hand traced the line of her jaw, shifting her into place for a thorough ravishing of her mouth. Amity moaned against his cheek as his rough fingertips stroked the curve of her neck. She pressed her body close to his seeking more.

"Oh. My. Lord."

The spell broke. Finlay loosened his grip around her waist. He sighed and reluctantly withdrew his hand from her cheek. Amity felt the loss of his touch, not unlike the moment she had first learned of her father and brother's deaths: with cold shock and devastation. Finn's kiss had reoriented her place in the world, and Amity would never be the same. She dragged her kiss-hazed gaze to meet Holly's furious glare. Immediately behind her stood Mrs. Mayweather, aghast.

"You *horrid* strumpet," Holly hissed. "Under my own roof, my own *cousin* seduces my intended fiancé."

Never mind that Wells House had once belonged to Amity's family. She knew every nook and cranny of this grand old pile. The familiar dings in the wainscoting along the music room, where she had gouged the wall with her bow during music lessons. The window seats in the library, where it was possible to lose oneself for days in histories and novels, back when books had not been a rarely affordable luxury. It had been her roof once too.

"Holly," Mrs. Mayweather snapped. Amity realized Finlay had moved to speak. To defend her, or to grovel to Holly? What might have he said to repair the damage, had Mrs. Mayweather not intervened? "Enough, child. A man is entitled to change his mind. I daresay you've expressed little interest in Mr. Weston until this very morning. It's hardly a wonder if he directs his affections elsewhere." Mrs. Mayweather narrowed her eyes at Amity. Her heart galloped like a frightened horse. "We presented you with three fine men seeking wives, not because we expected you to marry one of them but because we thought you might need a bit of assistance with finding a husband. I *never* could have anticipated that you, of all people, might make a claim upon my own daughter's intended."

And that did make her feel small. Greedy. Amity folded her hands behind her back and examined the pattern on the rug as if it were the most intriguing thing in the world. The others in the parlor craned their necks to see what the commotion was about.

"I...uh, believe there has been a misunderstanding," Finlay interjected. "Miss Mayweather happened to be standing beneath the mistletoe. I felt obliged to honor the spirit of the season."

Amity glanced up. Sure enough, green boughs with their red ribbons and white berries mocked her from above. They had shifted out of direct alignment with the greenery, but as excuses went, it wasn't bad. Mrs. Mayweather's expression transformed. Holly, however...

Kissing her cousin's husband-to-be had lit a pyre beneath their friendship. The hurt anger in Holly's blue eyes pierced Amity's heart with regret. It didn't matter that Finlay had not asked Holly to marry him yet. He had asked her father, which was arguably more serious. Had Amity alienated her family to win the heart of a man who had all but forgotten her since her brother's death?

Perhaps Amity had only seen what she'd wanted to.

"Is that so?" Mrs. Mayweather replied evenly, her eyes darting between their faces.

Amity had no doubt her cheeks were as scarlet as the ribbons hanging that wretched mistletoe. Nonetheless, she bobbed her head in agreement. "It meant nothing, Aunt Jane. Please understand I intended no harm."

"That's not what she said last night—"

"Holly. I believe our guests have tired of the entertainment. Will you please take your place at the pianoforte?"

"Mother—" Holly wailed in protest.

"Mr. Weston, if you will please join my daughter?" Mrs. Mayweather took Finlay by the arm. Amity mustered a wan smile as she watched him lean over the instrument beside Holly, the better to turn the pages of her sheet music.

Mr. Gibbs caught her eye and waggled his fingers her direction. Amity brushed away her feelings and managed to smile back. Not to be outdone, Mr. Lunt moved in her direction.

"Miss Mayweather, might I entice you into dancing a reel?" he asked.

Amity judged the chances of him attempting to kiss her again in full view of everyone as slim to none. Besides, it was in her favor to act as though nothing was wrong. Dancing with Lunt was the perfect way to demonstrate that the kiss with Finn had been more or less within the bounds of propriety.

That, more than anything, made the memory of their kiss feel dirty. It didn't matter that she had only been one half of the scandal. Amity bore all of the blame for their coequal transgression. She could rail against the fact all she wished, or she could remember her station in life, accept the consequences and move on. She had her sisters' futures to consider, after all.

"With great pleasure, Mr. Lunt." Amity offered the man her hand. He bowed over it, and they took their places for a country reel. A few minutes later, she was laughing a little too loudly as she skipped through the half-remembered steps. Finlay's dark blue gaze bore into her back. She cast him a fleeting glance. Frustration was etched in the flatness of his mouth and the furrow of his brow. He and Holly made a charming pair on the surface, but there was no warmth between them. Amity and Holly had agreed to let Finlay Weston choose his preferred bride. Holly clearly meant to have a proposal from him, but Amity was through with romantic manipulations. She had a single, perfect kiss to carry her through years of marriage to Gibbs or Lunt, or any other man.

One day, she might learn how not to want more of Finn's touch. Tonight, however, she had suitors to encourage.

Chapter Seven

"Are you planning to ask my daughter for her hand or not?" Mayweather demanded while they were out hunting—again—with Lunt and Gibbs three days later. Finn had managed to avoid asking Holly the most important question on his mind despite Holly's determined campaign to charm him into proposing. Now that Mrs. Mayweather's relatives had departed, the Foster Mayweather was losing patience with Finn.

"I am..." Finlay coughed. *Not.* He was not planning to offer for Holly at all. Not when the mere sight of Amity sent a confusing bolt of emotions through his body. "Getting to it."

Mayweather's brow creased into canyons of irritation. Finlay arched one eyebrow in return. He hadn't worked up the courage to inform his host of his decision yet. Once he did, he would undoubtedly be asked to leave—thus depriving him of Amity's company. Not that she had been any company at all over the past three days. Amity had been the closest thing to a ghost that Wells House possessed. When Finlay entered the drawing room, she bobbed a curtsey and took her leave. It left him with the sinking feeling that he had overstepped in kissing her. Her avoidance withered his pride and made him question the yearning he'd read in her green eyes.

Holly, on the other hand, stuck to his side like a burr. Yet, still, he didn't believe her abrupt shift in interest. He found it calculated and dishonest.

"See that you make it happen soon." Mayweather raised his weapon and fired. A moment later, he cursed. "Damn birds have learned not to rest easily when I am out with a gun and a dog." He grunted. "I can't understand it. Two weeks ago, in London, you were keen enough on Holly to seek my permission to marry her. I invited you to my home to give you ample time to get the job done. What's changed?"

Amity. "There has been a misunderstanding concerning the depths of my affections for your daughter," Finlay began. Meeting Amity again, as a woman, had shuffled his views on the necessity of affection to marriage. Until one week ago, he had blithely presumed all it took to make a successful union was a general compatibility with another human being by whom one wasn't utterly repulsed. Holly did not repulse him. Yet, away from the glamour and gossip of London, Finlay did not find Holly's company as appealing as when they had exchanged banter on crowded dance floors. She flirted with everyone. How would Holly manage long winters here in the countryside with no one to chatter at? She would drive him mad.

"Mayweather!" called out Gibbs from across the pond. "Come quickly! He's been shot!"

"Hold that thought, Weston." Mayweather plodded off through the fresh-fallen snow toward Gibbs. Finn followed. The sight of crimson droplets spattered over the snow quickened his pulse. The trail led to Lunt, who clutched his leg and moaned a few feet from the scene of the accident.

"He's been shot," Finlay breathed.

Lunt's face contorted with pain. Gibbs tried to assist the larger man to his feet, but he couldn't get enough leverage. Mayweather took his other arm and bent to haul him up. His face was pale and grim.

"We ought to look at the wound before moving him," Finlay declared. Mayweather stopped mid-shuffle to glare at him. Hot clouds of breath billowed from his nose and mouth.

"Are you a doctor, now, Mr. Weston?" he demanded.

"No. It is common sense." Finlay bent to examine Lunt's leg. The man cried out when he touched a pulpy knot. "There's buckshot buried in his leg. We shall need clean utensils and rags, and a closer examination once we're inside." He stood up and brushed the snow from his thighs. "The bone does not appear to be broken. Can you make it back the house?"

With some struggle and a great deal of collective cursing, they flailed through the snow up the hill. The children gathered wide-eyed around the kitchen, where they deposited Lunt's ashen-faced form. They divested themselves of their outerwear. Blood dripped onto the wood plank floor.

"Eww," declared one of the children.

Mrs. Mayweather gasped. "What happened?"

"Your husband shot me," Mr. Lunt responded sharply.

"I never meant to," Mayweather defended himself. "It was an accident. I was aiming at a duck."

"I am quite a lot larger than a damned duck!" Lunt roared, in agony as the housekeeper and Mrs. Mayweather propped his leg on the next chair and began to cut away the fabric of his trousers. Holly set about helping the maids gather clean linens to bind the wound.

In the commotion, Finlay found his opportunity to slip away. It was a grievous injury but there was little he could do for the moment, apart from stand by gawking at the unfortunate man. Finlay needed to know Amity's true feelings toward him before he burned bridges with Mayweather. While he despised himself as less than a gentleman for desiring to back out of the agreed-upon marriage, the thought of Amity married to either of her suitors—to any man but him—gutted him.

Amity wasn't in the music room, nor was she in the parlor. Finlay tiptoed past the kitchen to see whether Lunt's bellowing had brought her out of hiding, but it hadn't. Nor was she reading with the children…

The library. Finlay's face stretched into a grin. At this time of year, the servants didn't set a fire until late in the evening, if the men chose to retire there instead of to Mayweather's study for post-supper cordials. Amity had always loved to spend hours with her nose in a book. Finlay eased open the heavy oak door to discover…emptiness.

"Amity?" he asked, his voice echoing off the long rows of gilt-embossed leather-bound books. They mostly matched, for the Mayweathers had the luxury of sending out new books to be custom bound. A finger of unease touched Finlay's neck as he wondered again how the Mayweather women had fared since their unfortunate removal from Wells house. Why hadn't he thought to do more than send an occasional letter to the family around the time of Ellis's death?

Because it had been too painful for him to bear. When Finn had lost his father, lazy summers had given way to learning to manage the family estate at his father's steward's side, under his mother's fretful eye.

A scuffle from behind him brought Finlay out of his self-recrimination. Ah, yes. The window seats. A quilt corner slithered between two heavy velvet curtains. If that had not been confirmation enough of Amity's presence, the fact that a single window was covered against the wan winter light did.

Finlay's heart skipped a beat as he went over to the

window and knocked on the frame. "Amity. I know you're in there."

The curtains parted. The tip of Amity's nose and below her bright eyes peered up at him. "I heard shouting a while ago. Is everything all right?"

"One of your suitors was shot by accident."

"Oh." Her eyes widened. "Which one?"

"Lunt."

"Ah. I trust he shall recover?" she asked with no more concern than was appropriate for an acquaintance. Amity had made a little bed for herself in the cramped window seat. It was even colder between the curtains and the casement windows. Her ears and nose were pink with the chill. She had wrapped the blanket around her legs and pulled it up to her chin. A book lay open, facedown, across her knees.

"Assuming the shot was clean and the wound doesn't turn septic, I expect he shall have nothing but a scar for a souvenir in a few months' time." Finlay glanced down, then back at Amity. What if she did not return his affections? Perhaps he had been the one to latch on to his old friend in a mistaken case of cold feet before making the most momentous decision of his life.

But then Amity's gaze met his, and heat flared through his body. He read sadness and worry behind the forced cheer of the rest of her expression. "Amity," he asked huskily, "what's wrong?"

Amity hung her head and choked back a sob. "I miss my sisters," she whispered after a minute. Collecting herself, Amity sat up straight and leaned against the wood. The quilt fell down her body to reveal the rise of her bosom covered by a pale-yellow dress that had faded to the color of old tea stains. Finlay swallowed.

"Are you planning to leave early?"

Amity scoffed. "No, of course not. Any of my sisters

would love to be here in my place. Any one of them would better appreciate the attentions from Mr. Lunt and Mr. Gibbs."

"Have you resolved to refuse them, should they offer?"

"Mr. Gibbs asked for my hand this morning," Amity replied glumly.

A vise tightened around Finlay's temples. Cold moisture beaded along the small of his back. "May I inquire as to your reply?"

"'Tis out of line for you to do so, and you know it, Finlay Weston." Amity tugged the quilt over her shoulders like a cotton shield. "Nonetheless, we are old friends, aren't we?" she asked wistfully. "I don't mind confiding that I was not prepared to accept any man's proposal on such short acquaintance."

Relief loosened the crushing pressure around Finlay's head so abruptly that he felt lightheaded.

"And you, Mr. Weston? Have you made my cousin the happiest of women?" Amity picked at a loose thread as though it was the most fascinating object in all the world, although her cheeks took on a brighter hue of pink. A spot in the center of his chest warmed.

"I find I cannot bring myself to ask for her hand, Amity."

Her chin jerked up. The desolation in her eyes had been replaced by wary hope. "Why not?"

"Because I find my affections have been utterly stolen by her bitter rival. You, Amity."

"Me?" she squeaked, shifting upward. "Oh, this is terrible."

"Terrible?" Confused, Finlay could summon no better response that to repeat her.

Amity kicked back the blanket and swung her legs down to the cold floor. To his consternation, Finn glimpsed the smooth curve of her calf above mended stockings that had sagged woefully around her ankles. Amity crouched to yank them into place, giving him another view of her undergarments. Stained. Patched. Unfit for the luscious curve of her buttocks, lovingly highlighted by material worn thin from use and washing.

"Yes, it's not to be borne, Finn. You know if we are caught together here, I shall be ruined. Me. Not you. I cannot afford to let that happen."

The Mayweathers hadn't just lost their home, he realized. They had lost their income and status. The entirety of their daily life had been swept away with a single awful wreck. All Amity had was her reputation and her family connections. It was the height of selfishness for him to threaten the little security she had. If only he could go back in time and kick his cock-sure self in the arse for deciding upon Holly after a few weeks' acquaintance, simply because she was beautiful and convenient.

"I won't let that happen, Amity," Finlay declared.

Amity hauled the quilt up around her shoulders like a bulky shawl. Finlay captured the corners and used it to pin her arms down as he clasped the edges tight beneath her chin, currently leveled at a defiant angle. "Oh? How exactly do you intend to prevent it?" Amity demanded, but her gaze rested on his mouth, and Finlay knew she was thinking about the kiss. Their glorious, wonderful kiss beneath the mistletoe.

"By marrying you, Amity," he whispered and pulled her against his chest.

Chapter Eight

Amity laughed. "The devil you will."

"Amity," Finn groaned against her mouth. "If I can't convince you with words, let me show you with kisses."

She was tired of resisting him. For days, she had kept clear of Finlay in hopes that she and Holly could resolve their differences. It hadn't worked. Each hour had deepened the trench between them until Amity feared they had crossed into outright enmity. She deserved a little joy this holiday. More than just at Christmas—Amity deserved the warm happiness that had helped Mother survive devastating loss.

She couldn't stand to be a secondary consideration in her cousin's ambitions. Holly wanted Finlay, but he no longer wanted her in return. Finn had chosen *her*. Amity. The knowledge lifted a heavy weight within her.

Alone, at least for a brief while, she could reach for the future she wanted but dared not grasp. Amity stretched up on tiptoe to close the distance between them. Her lips met his in an ardent embrace. Amity's legs turned rubbery. If this was to be the only time they had together, she resolved to enjoy every moment. She shimmied out of the confines of her quilt to wrap both arms around his neck.

"I thought I could be noble," she gasped between kisses. "I thought I could surrender you to Holly. But I can't. I want to keep you for myself."

"Shh. Do not summon your cousin," Finn whispered.

Amity's mouth gaped as his hand skimmed up her ribs. Finn's thumb traced the underside of her breast. Amity's back arched instinctively, seeking more. "Yes," she hissed.

Finn sucked her lower lip, which sent a ripple of pleasure through Amity's body. Time fell away. Past became present. Amity shuddered at his touch. The future dimmed. Perhaps it had never been very bright. Amity could not mourn a future that asked her to tie herself bodily to a man she did not desire. Her soul refused to concede—she would have pleasure, or she would have nothing. She could only hope her sisters would understand why she had wasted her mother's gift.

He wants to marry you. But wasn't that what all men said before they took advantage of a woman?

Amity's hunger had her leaning into Finlay's touch like a purring barn cat. Finn palmed her breast. His erect cock jutted against her stomach through layers of clothing. He wanted her in return. The knowledge thrilled her.

"Do that, more," she gasped. Finlay obliged. He dropped both hands to her waist and leaned back to lift her against his chest. The scratch of wool and rough glide of linen over the tops of her breasts sent liquid heat streaking through her veins. Amity tried to wrap her legs around his waist but was thwarted by the narrow cut of her dress. The skirt trapped her legs closed.

"Finn," Amity half-groaned, "Set me down."

"Fine," he grunted between desperate kisses. He perched her on the edge of the window seat and stood back, panting, his hair mussed, his cravat wrinkled and his jacket askew. Finlay half glowered at her, his angular features echoing all the emotions Amity didn't know how to express. Mere words seemed insufficient to the task.

An unfamiliar knowing took hold of Amity, an understanding that she appeared just as disheveled. If she was only to have one opportunity to feel these things in her lifetime, why not with a man she trusted to keep their secret after the act of lovemaking was done?

Perhaps Finn meant his spurious offer of marriage, but Amity didn't believe it. Gentlemen did not court one woman and then abruptly decide to marry another, no matter how longstanding their acquaintance. She had known Finlay Weston, the man, for less than a week.

"If you were mine," she whispered her heart's greatest wish, "I would let you push my skirts up and touch my most secret place."

"Amity," Finn groaned as he complied with her spoken desire. "If you were mine, I would burn your underthings and buy you the finest lace chemise in England. I would ask you to wear it and nothing else. Your breasts—" he palmed one as he spoke, and Amity was overcome with desire, "—would be visible beneath the fine mesh. I could savor their rosy tips any time I desired."

"Touch me," she pleaded. Her skirt and chemise had bunched up around her thighs, leaving her legs free to fall open.

"If you were mine, Amity," Finn replied huskily, "I would take you to bed before sunset and not let you sleep until well after midnight. Do you understand my meaning?"

Amity dug her fingers into the slippery dark strands of hair at the nape his neck. Eyes hooded, Finn bent to swirl his tongue around the taut bud he had poked above the barrier of her bodice. Amity gasped and urged him closer. "Yes. If you were mine, Finn, I would keep you abed long past sunrise. I would run my tongue along your ear, like this." She demonstrated with the light scratch of one fingernail. He shuddered.

"If you were mine, Amity," Finn whispered against her breasts as his hands worked the laces at her side, "your ears would ache from the weight of the gems I would hang from this delicate lobe."

"Yes." Amity shuddered as he sucked her soft flesh, then pressed a row of kisses down the thread pulse in her throat. As long as he kept kissing and sucking her like this, she could agree to almost anything. *She would abandon her family and ruin her reputation—just please keep flicking your tongue over my nipple.* Her thoughts disintegrated as Finn managed to poke the tips of her breasts above the tight binding of her bodice. They pulled into tight beads the instant they were exposed to the bracing chill. "Keep doing that," she breathed. Amity leaned back against the glass. Shame for the poor state of her underthings almost stopped her. But the fierce desire in Finn's dark eyes set her body aflame with need.

"Amity," he growled. "You intoxicate me. I am desperate to taste you."

"Taste me?" she questioned breathlessly, although Amity had an idea of what he meant.

"Here," he clarified, stroking her sex with blunt fingers. Amity whimpered with want.

"Yes. More. I like that," she babbled. Finlay's cravat crumpled in her hands, loose enough to reveal his Adam's apple and a hint of his chest. "I wish we were naked. Together."

"I am yet a gentleman, Amity," Finlay warned. Before her fractured brain could parse his meaning, he fell to his knees before her. "I am not going to be gentlemanly now."

"Please," Amity begged, not knowing precisely what he meant to do but aching with need. Finlay's lips stretched into a smirk.

"Anything you wish, love." He turned serious as he rolled the node at the apex of her core between his fingers.

Amity gasped and bucked, seeking more. He gave it, exploring her slick passage with one finger, then two. She grabbed his hair for dear life as pleasure tightened her body. "More, Finn. I need more."

"Soon," he whispered, curling his fingertips upward. She was so close to the fleeting joy of climax, which she had never experienced with another person. Only her lonely self, in stolen moments alone in the shared bedroom at Kearny. This was grander, harsher, more powerful.

And that was before Finlay bent to lick the bud of her arousal the way he'd done with her earlobe. Amity released a harsh gasp. "Yes. Like that."

He complied, exploring, tasting her, running the tip of his tongue over her until a pulse of pleasure bloomed through her. Amity surrendered to it. She reached for the orgasm that left her spent, chasing it until it faded. Irretrievable.

There was a shuffle of fabric as Finlay set her clothing to rights. When Amity had recovered enough to sit up, she found damp tears on her cheeks.

Finlay had retreated, regret etched over his features. "If you were mine, Amity," he said on a sigh, "I would never let you go."

❄

As a precaution, Finlay departed the library several minutes before Amity. There was no need for stealth, however. No maid had interrupted the passion that still sent ripples through Amity's core. No footman had observed them entering the library, nor leaving it. There would be no public discovery to force Finn into proposing. Amity wanted him—badly—but not under duress.

He caught her hand to squeeze her fingers as she turned to climb the stairs to the guest quarters. "Shall I see you at supper?" Finn asked, his eyes searching her face.

Amity smiled down at him from the stairway. "I am fond of eating, and there is nowhere else for me to find sustenance. So, yes."

"If you were mine," he whispered, "I would never make you dress for dinner."

Amity felt her entire face flush all the way down to her toes. "Scandalous."

"I'd have trays brought to our rooms so we could spend more time—"

"There you are!" Holly's falsely bright voice interrupted. "I have been looking everywhere for you, Mr. Weston."

Finlay's expression shuttered. Amity's spine stiffened. She snatched her hand back as if it had been singed in a blacksmith's forge. She hardly dared to meet her cousin's gaze. For the brief moment she did, Amity read betrayal. Shame scorched through her.

Would you alienate your cousin's affections for a man who cannot make up his mind to which woman he will declare his intentions? After all, Holly's letters and descriptions of her life in London had been a small source of excitement in the years since Amity's uncle and aunt had taken possession of Wells House. Holly was the one who had given her a writing set and ribbons for her sisters, purchased with her pin money.

Finlay had written a couple of cursory notes, years ago, and then forgotten them.

"Cousin," Holly said coldly.

Amity nodded. She did not wish to fight, but what else had she done ever since Finlay had arrived and Amity had fallen tits over teakettles for her brother's best friend? "Holly," Amity said meekly. "I wish you much happiness in the coming year. Will you play a duet with me tonight after supper?"

Her cousin cast her a wary look. "Perhaps."

Amity did not look at Finlay. Perhaps this had all been a mistake. Maybe her time with him had been nothing but a Twelfth Night fantasy.

If Finlay wanted her for his wife, he would have to take the shine off his sterling reputation as a gentleman and tell Holly he no longer intended to propose.

*If you were mine...*but he wasn't. Not yet.

Chapter Nine

Spiced cider curdled unpleasantly in Finlay's stomach. The ground had shifted between him and Amity this afternoon. For one glorious hour, he had believed in their *if you were mine* exchanges. Then Holly had appeared, and in a split second, Amity had turned against him. It made him wonder whether he understood her at all. The woman she had become, not the girl she'd been. Amity the girl had been so adventurous. When had her meek reticence emerged? He hungered to fill the gaps in his knowledge of her life.

At midnight, Mrs. Mayweather threw open the front and back doors to Wells House. The women, led by Mrs. Mayweather and Holly, chased the spirits through the rooms of the first floor to invite good luck. They slammed the doors, laughing.

"Ridiculous tradition!" Mr. Mayweather huffed. "A waste of good firewood too." His cheeks were red with too much brandy and spiced ale. Lunt sat nearby, propped up on the sofa and picking at a tray of ginger snaps. The two men appeared to have mended fences. Thick white strips of linen encased Lunt's leg.

Only Finlay seemed unable to chase away the muted sadness that had settled over him after his afternoon interlude with Amity in the library. If she were his... But she never would be unless he spoke up and risked damaging his relationship with his closest neighbor.

Over a *woman*.

Every sensible fiber of his being railed against the wisdom of spoiling such an important friendship. A gentleman did not go back on his word, no matter how desperately he wanted a woman.

Amity's green eyes met his briefly. If Holly possessed the talent of the keys, Amity possessed a singing voice fit for angels. *"We twa hae run about the braes / and pou'd the gowans fine; / But we've wander'd mony a weary fit / sin' auld lang syne."*

Memories tumbled through his mind as the words' meaning in plain English raised specters of his youth. *We two have run about the slopes...* Amity's bright green eyes and snub nose morphed in his memory. *And picked the daisies fine...* The chains of white flowers morphed into orange blossoms and a veil in Finlay's imagination.

Finlay choked, coughed and rejoined his voice to the song. New memories crowded out the old. Amity's hooded green eyes darkened with lust as he, on his knees, teased her quim with his tongue. Her pants of pleasure as he explored her body with trembling hands. Lust rolled through him. He closed his eyes against the tide of feelings.

Should auld acquaintance be forgot, and never brought to mind? Should auld acquaintance be forgot, and auld lang syne?

He had forgotten Amity too long. As the final notes faded, Mrs. Mayweather laid her hand on his arm.

"I am so looking forward to introducing you as my future

son-in-law at our Twelfth Night ball in a few days," she said warmly, sotto voce. "I trust you won't dash Holly's hopes."

Finlay swallowed. By the time he disengaged from his hostess's embrace, Amity had ensconced herself on the sofa next to Lunt. She cradled her mug like a dragon guarding treasure as they conversed with heads bent close. He clenched his fists at his side. Across the room, Gibbs sulked as he played cards with Mrs. Mayweather's elderly aunt. No doubt Amity had been avoiding the man.

Good. It bought Finlay a bit more time to speak with Foster Mayweather about proposing to Amity instead of Holly. It would be uncomfortable, but if necessary, he could retreat to his neighboring home, Weston Manor. Even with the staff on paid holiday while the masons shored up crumbling stonework, Finlay could pass a warm enough Twelfth Night knowing he could look forward to claiming Amity as his bride.

"Excuse me," Mrs. Mayweather said loudly and clapped to get the crowd's attention. "I have an announcement."

Amity and Lunt sat next to one another on the settee. Her hands were clasped in her lap, gaze glued to the floor, her cheeks stained pink. Foreboding slowed time as Finlay absorbed Mrs. Mayweather's speech.

"Mr. Lunt and my niece by marriage, Miss Amity Mayweather, have agreed to marry."

No. Time stopped. Cold horror washed through Finlay's body.

"So much for refusing to accept a proposal from any man on short acquaintance," muttered Gibbs furiously from across the room. His face had turned a mottled red of alcohol and indignation. "Or is it only me you couldn't abide?" Affronted, Gibbs stomped out of the room.

Silence descended for a beat in his wake. Finally, Amity raised her eyes to meet his. Guilt. Regret.

Finlay shook his head as understanding cleaved his heart into two. He had dithered too long. Still, anger surged within him. How dare she give her body to him, and then promise her heart to another?

Well. Just because his oldest friend had rejected him in favor of a boorish lummox didn't mean Finlay had to endure the rest of this evening alone. He broke gazes with Amity. It felt like tearing his beating heart out with his bare hands, but he could not look at Lunt's smug possessiveness for another second.

With two strides, he was at the piano. Holly's bright blue gaze met his, twinkling with delight. "Might I have a private word?"

"Anything you have to say can be spoken in front of my family. Besides, no one is paying us any attention, except my cousin." Holly's voice flattened, and her mouth tightened at the corners with disappointment.

Fine. If Holly wanted him to propose in front of everyone here, he would do so. "Holly Mayweather, would you do me the great honor of becoming my wife?"

Holly cocked her head. "Um..." Her eyes darted to Amity, whose embarrassment had faded and left her cheeks drained of color. She looked miserable. "I am cognizant of the great compliment you have given me. However, I regret I must decline."

"I beg your pardon?"

"I do not accept your offer of marriage," Holly replied with impish pity. "I fear my heart is given elsewhere."

"But...but why?" Finlay sputtered. "Why did you lead me to believe you welcomed my advances?"

"Do we have another happy announcement?" asked Mrs. Mayweather expectantly as she glided toward them.

"I am afraid not. Your daughter has rejected my offer,"

Finlay declared bitterly. By now, the entire room was watching. His humiliation was complete.

"Holly Mayweather," her mother warned. Her ringlets trembled at her temples. "What are you doing?"

"Papa told me he wouldn't pay for my fourth season in London unless I proved that I might find a suitor. Now that I have demonstrated my ability to attract a proposal when I wish to receive one, Papa must let me return." Holly grinned sweetly and leaned back on the edge of the pianoforte.

"This is about that rake, Lord Stockton, isn't it," Mrs. Mayweather declared in a tight hiss like an angry goose, trying to keep her voice low and failing.

Finlay groaned. "You cannot be serious, Holly."

"I beg your pardon," the lady who had rejected him so publicly echoed back at him. Her chin jolted upward a full inch. For one awful moment, Finlay hated her.

"If you think Stockton will ever seek your hand as wife, Miss Mayweather," he said with all the amusement he could muster, "you are utterly deluded."

Holly's gaze narrowed into slits. "Does it wound your pride that I aim higher than your admittedly enviable station, Mr. Weston?"

He laughed. The shining, unmitigated gall of this woman. "Not in the least. You have spared me the long consequences of what would have been an unfortunate match, had you accepted me." Finlay bowed. "I find the tradition of chasing out bad spirits has left a few behind. I shall take the remaining demons with me." He turned on his heel. Everyone in the room was riveted upon the scene playing out beside the lacquered pianoforte. Everyone except Amity. "Summon my valet," he ordered a footman, who scrambled to comply. "I depart in a quarter hour."

Silence blanketed the room. Finlay couldn't look at either of the women who had so betrayed him. He stomped toward the door as flustered as he had been upon his arrival. The New Year of 1817 would go down as the worst ever in his personal history books.

"Wait, Finlay, I—" Amity rushed after him.

Finlay had no further appetite for scandal, however. "Miss Mayweather, I wish you great happiness in your forthcoming nuptials."

Amity regarded him as though he had slapped her straight across the cheek.

❄

As Finlay exited in a huff of wounded masculine pride, Amity reeled from more than a few sips of cider and a too-warm, too-crowded room. For an hour she managed to hold herself together. Lunt touched her constantly. When Amity eased her hand out of his grasp, the man slipped his arm about her shoulders. She shifted away and found his uninjured leg pressed against her side.

Amity hadn't meant to accept him. After their interlude in the library, she had expected Finlay to make some kind of gentlemanly gesture, even if it wasn't an offer of marriage. But tonight, he had scarcely acknowledged her presence. Lunt had caught her off-guard with his "Will you consider doing me the honor of becoming my wife?"

"Yes," she had replied, half listening, her mind focused on the word "consider." *Consideration* meant time to mull the idea, in her view. Certainly, it meant more time than a single evening—but once her overexcited beau had whispered the news to Amity's aunt, the misunderstanding had crystalized into fact before she'd had time to consider Lunt's proposal. Her love was not limited to a single man; she had sisters to consider. If Finlay wasn't going to offer for her, and the alternative was to accept Gibbs, then Lunt's proposal was as good as she could expect. A woman in reduced circumstances ought to be grateful for any offer of marriage she received.

But she could never bring herself to be happy. It was all she could do not to physically recoil from Lunt's touch.

The man whose touch melted her core, however, had regarded her with blue eyes turned to icicles. Her heart had frozen over at the accusation she'd found in Finlay's scowl. What had she done? The responsible thing. The *right* thing, even if nothing felt right about it at all. He, of all people, ought to understand the meaning of honor and self-sacrifice.

Yet here she was in her mother's ruined bedsheet dress adorned with lace from a baby's christening gown. Amity had known the afternoon spent in Finlay's arms was never to be repeated. *If you were mine…*

But he wasn't.

Finlay had turned away from her and toward Holly. With their heads bent together over the pianoforte, it had been clear there was a very serious conversation going on. Most of the guests hadn't cared—at least, not until Amity's aunt had made a fuss over Holly's rejection.

Amity cornered her cousin just outside the parlor. "Why did you do that?"

Holly cast her a cool, sidelong glance before straightening her shawl. "You know why. I love Stockton."

"You might have said something sooner," Amity chided.

"I did, Amity. I would have told you about my father's stipulation that I receive one proposal before I am allowed to return to town for another season, had I thought you would pursue Mr. Weston."

"What?" Amity's mouth popped open in a

"You, cousin, have become shy and meek in the years since we last met." Holly swept down the hall in a very countess-like fashion. Her head jerked to indicate that Amity was to follow. "After our talk in my bedroom, I thought for certain that you were going to let Finlay know you wanted him instead of passively waiting for him to come to you. Men like women with a bit of fight in them. No one wishes to spend their life with a limp rag."

"I am not a limp rag," Amity protested hotly. "If I may be truthful, Holly, London has transformed you into a calculating, capricious flirt, *dear* cousin."

"At least I know how to interact with gentlemen," Holly replied indignantly. "It's as if entertaining a gentleman's attentions is a foreign concept to you. I suggest you take pointers from me before you are indisputably on the shelf."

"Pointers." Amity scoffed. "From you."

They came to Holly's bedroom door. "Suit yourself, Amity. Finlay will have no difficulty finding a replacement for me. A replacement for you will not be so simple."

"You cannot expect me to dash over to Weston Manor and ask Finn to marry me. What of Lunt?"

"I expect you ought to say something before he posts the banns," Holly remarked as she fiddled with her key. The lock clicked open. She yawned. A clock down the hallway struck an hour past midnight. "Mr. Lunt doesn't strike me as the type of man to take rejection lightly."

"Finlay isn't either," Amity declared.

Holly shrugged. "If you wish Mr. Weston to be your concern, I recommend you tell him as much—and advise Lunt of your change in affections. If you'll excuse me." Holly sketched a curtsey. "I find this evening has taxed me greatly."

Chapter Ten

Escaping her accidental engagement to Lunt proved more difficult than extracting one's boot from bog muck.

"Do you ever intend to speak up?" asked Holly the night her mother's relatives returned for the Twelfth Night ball. The poor harvests this year meant few families were hosting the customary grand balls. Even the lord and lady of Willoughby Hall, the finest residence in Hertfordshire, had declined to hold a ball this year. With the infusion of more guests, Amity had once again lost her private guest room. Back in Holly's bedroom, the cousins sniped and needled one another. It was far less pleasant than the gushing happiness that had marked their initial reunion—but to Amity, the newfound honesty was refreshing.

"Concerning Lunt?" Amity dragged a brush through her stick-straight hair.

"For a start," Holly replied tartly as she examined the contents of her wardrobe. "This would suit you."

"I told you, I'm wearing the blue and gold."

"That dress is woefully out of date and badly faded. We are similar in height. Please borrow one of mine, Amity. No? Well, I suppose it doesn't matter if Finlay Weston isn't going to attend. This is far too fine for the likes of Lunt. Your blue and gold suits him fine." Holly had given up any effort to conceal her exasperation.

"Has Finlay responded to your mother's letter?" Amity asked, picking at her nightgown. Mrs. Mayweather had forced Holly to write an apology for rejecting him so rudely. The footman had returned with a hastily dispatched note that Finlay held no ill feelings toward Miss Mayweather and wished her much success in winning Stockton's heart. Mrs. Mayweather, sensing hope, had immediately dispatched a second letter to assure Finlay that he was still welcome to attend the Mayweather's Twelfth Night party, if he could find it within his heart to forgive the insult. Their frozen footman had returned an hour later with news that Mr. Weston had departed the hall in a great hurry only a few hours since. Despite daily inquiries as to his return, the workers had no further information—only the peculiar news that several of the household staff had been recalled to the property earlier than expected. The masons and plasterers had been asked to hasten repairs on the interior in preparation for arriving guests in before Twelfth Night.

Holly shook her head. "No. Everyone is most perplexed." She tapped her fingertip against her lower lip. "Weston House wasn't expected to be ready until the springtime. It is odd that he should disappear so abruptly. To say he's expecting guests…what could he mean by that? Is he planning to throw a rival ball?"

Amity snorted. "Is that what your mother thinks?"

"It's precisely the sort of thing she would believe." Holly nodded sagely. "My parents like to pretend my dramatic impulses are unique, but my mother will tell anyone who listens how I take after her. She has undoubtedly invited half the countryside in a bid to prevent him from having any guests at all."

"As though we can fit another family here at Wells House," Amity scoffed. "It's packed to the rafters. Even the carriage house has been remade into lodgings for the Mayweather families."

"It's too bad that so many of the new arrivals are Mayweather relations," Holly remarked with a glimmer of mischief in her eye. "Otherwise, you might have an easier time finding a replacement for Lunt."

Amity tossed an embroidered cushion at her cousin's head and nearly took out the lamp. Her heart ached with confusion. She missed Finlay's steadfast presence. If she knew where he'd gone, she might commandeer a horse and footman to go after him. But he had simply disappeared, leaving her to wonder whether he had ever cared about her beyond a kiss beneath the mistletoe and an hour of happiness in a cold library.

❋

"We must change horses, my lord." His driver's teeth chattered as he spoke. Curse the unbearably cold weather that made the drive take twice as long as usual. Thick, unyielding snowdrifts were piled up at the sides of the road, replenished hourly with new falls of fat snowflakes.

"Come inside," Finlay demanded. "I shall take your place." Cold bit his cheeks the instant he exited the relative warmth of his smallest, lightest carriage. The horses trudged on, dejected, their flanks twitching. Finlay stopped them to pull extra blankets from the boot and tuck them snugly around the horse's backs. They went on. There was nothing else for them to do. To stop in this storm meant freezing to death—and Finlay had too much to live for. He had to get back to Amity before it was too late.

❄

"Mr. Lunt," Amity interrupted—again.

"I should like to wed within the month, as soon as the banns have had time to post. Will that be enough time for you to prepare?" her putative fiancé asked, which was a bit better than half an hour ago when he had simply informed her about his plans to make her his wife. Marriage negotiations had been simple. She did not wish to marry him. There was no agreement to reach—not until her mother had had a chance to speak with Amity's prospective suitor.

"Mr. Lunt, I cannot proceed with any planning without my mother's direct involvement." Amity had a strong feeling her mother would agree to anything Mr. Lunt desired if it meant some relief from their grinding poverty.

Lunt's thick eyebrows crawled together like wooly caterpillars. "But I have reached a settlement with your uncle."

Anger flashed through Amity. "My uncle does not speak for me. My mother does."

"Amity, love."

Oh, not this again. She hated the way Lunt had taken to using the endearment over the past four days. He used it strategically to make it more difficult for her to break off with him. As though she wasn't finding it difficult enough.

A few feet away, Holly pretended not to eavesdrop as she smiled and nodded at the Mayweather aunts and cousins who had arrived that morning. They could not stop complaining about having been delayed by the heavy snowfall. Mrs.

Mayweather had agreed to host the new arrivals until well after Twelfth Night in recompense. Amity's uncle had taken to worrying openly about the expense of hosting so many visitors for so long, in a year when their income had been devastated by the blanket of cold that covered England.

"Mr. Lunt, I beg you refrain from calling me by that term," Amity said a little more sharply than she had intended to.

"We are to be married," Lunt pointed out. "He shall settle one hundred pounds upon you upon marriage, and another fifty pounds per annum for five years thereafter."

"Am I to be sold so cheaply?" Amity inhaled deeply, her breasts pressing hard against the bodice of the day dress she had borrowed from Holly. "If I am to sign away my life to a man, it will be one for whom I have feelings. Not one who used an injury to play upon my sympathies and press me into making a public announcement before securing my affections. How could I feel anything but resentment toward you under the circumstances, Mr. Lunt?"

A shocked silence fell over the room. Mrs. Mayweather's expression turned serious, then exasperated. Holly, alone, beamed at her.

"I cannot have a second marriage rejected in my own parlor in the space of a week, Amity Mayweather." Her aunt advanced upon her. The many offshoots of the Mayweather clan dispersed in every direction, only to fill the path behind her, craning their necks in curiosity. "The world will think Wells House is where love goes to die."

"Mama," Holly interjected, popping up to stand next to Amity. "Perhaps you should have considered our wishes before pressing us to marry where our hearts were not given, if you wished to guard your reputation as matchmaker."

Amity gathered her courage, though slick anxiety turned

her skin clammy. "I thank you and my uncle not to interfere where you have not been asked to help. Was my mother not to be consulted in my decision to marry?"

"Your mother is too soft-hearted to be trusted with your future, Amity. Can't you see that?" Mr. Mayweather declared. "We offered to bring her to London, where she might find a suitable new husband. But no, Laura Mayweather was too enamored of my brother to ever countenance remarriage."

The scorn in his voice made Amity see red. "Is this what you do to everyone? Arrange their lives for them without regard to their feelings or consent?"

"Yes," interjected Holly. Her parents glared.

"You, of all people, need more direction than most," huffed Mrs. Mayweather. "As though Lord Stockton will ever offer for you."

"I cannot tell you how greatly I appreciate your confidence in my prospects, Mother. Besides which, it is better than marriage to a man who is in love with my *cousin*," Holly shot back. Tears glimmered in her eyes, but judging from the stubborn tilt of her chin, her cousin would be damned before letting them fall.

"At least Mr. Weston possesses a fortune and the cool head to manage it properly," shouted Mr. Mayweather.

In that moment, she chose to forgive her cousin's manipulations. Holly had been instructed in the social art of deviousness from the cradle—and without her cousin's intervention, Amity might never have fought for Finlay's love. "That is no reason to bargain me away," Amity pointed out with all the calmness she could muster. Standing up to Lunt had not come naturally, but she had done it, and pride blossomed in her bosom.

"Bargain you away?" Mr. Lunt interjected, pulling himself awkwardly onto the crutch he was using until his leg healed enough to walk on. "Some bargain. I have never been so insulted as to be dismissed by a young woman with no fortune, a middling-fair face and no future prospects to speak of. Mr. Weston may *have* you, Amity," Lunt said bitterly as he crutched toward the doorway as rapidly as he could maneuver through the crowd of Mayweather relatives. "That is, if he ever comes back."

Chapter Eleven

Thus, the Mayweather's Twelfth Night ball commenced with an edge of unease—at least for Amity and Holly, who huddled near the fireplace, pariahs, as other young ladies played the pianoforte. Nobody asked them to dance.

"I never meant to cause such a scandal," Amity whispered, horrified at the part she had played in the debacle of the evening.

"The scandal is not you. It isn't me, either. It is my parents," Holly replied darkly. "We are only bit players in this family drama." She had dressed in pale cream silk embroidered with pink and beaded with tiny seed pearls. Larger pearls decorated the fashionable curls that dangled to her shoulders like fat sausages. Her expression was one of determined good cheer, but when she spoke, her face fell, and tiny crescents formed at the corners of her mouth. She clutched the reticule Amity had made for her in one hand as if preparing to swing it at the first person to mention marriage.

Everyone apart from Holly and Amity appeared to be having a fine time. The extravagant Twelfth Cake stood regally in the center of a small, round table placed in the empty sitting room just off the parlor. Rather than destroy the lovely creation too early, Mr. and Mrs. Mayweather had passed out small cards with roles printed upon them. To everyone's great amusement, the butler had drawn the King card and must be treated accordingly through endless games of charades.

Neither Holly nor Amity had been offered a card.

Where is Finlay?

Thoughts of marriage had flown straight out of Amity's head once Lunt had spoken the unthinkable words that Finlay Weston was gone. The brewing scandal had begun to coalesce around the notion that he had been devastated by Holly's spurning of his suit and retreated into hiding. Holly, as practical-minded as she was independent, rolled her eyes at this.

But Amity could not stop her the sense of unease. It would be just like Finlay Weston to disappear on some great errand and die in a snowbank, alone—without her there to save him, all because she had lost courage at the wrong moment. In retrospect, Lunt's proposal had been as repulsive as his kiss beneath the mistletoe. Ill-timed. Undesired. Overbearing.

He had played upon her sympathies to push her into a marriage and, worse, Amity had let him. Her eyes darted to the door with greater and greater frequency as the night dragged on.

"He's not coming," Holly whispered sympathetically. "Between me and my parents, I doubt Mr. Weston will ever set foot in Wells House again."

Amity sipped her wassail, which had grown cold and tasted of old apples. "I cannot blame him. I may never return to Wells House, either. Not even for you."

"We must remain here slapping away children's hands

until the Twelfth Cake is served," Holly observed grimly, a smile pasted over her face. "After that, I shall help you pack. I don't suppose you'd consider bringing me with you?"

"Are you fond of raising chickens?" Amity asked skeptically. Curls bouncing, Holly shook her head in a mute no. "It won't get you back to London and your Lord Stockton, either."

"At least you shall have an ending to this painful mess, unlike myself. I am certain he cares for me. I only need to see him—"

A gust of cold air made the roaring fire sputter.

"Mrs. Mayweather, Miss Charity Mayweather, Miss Mary Anne Mayweather, Miss Leticia Mayweather," announced a servant.

Blood drained from Amity's face. "Mother," she whispered. What on earth had possessed her family to come all this way in such horrid weather?

"And Mr. Finlay Weston," continued the servant.

Amity froze midrush toward her family. The room stilled. Her heart lurched into her throat. She fell into his dark gaze. "Finn," she whispered.

"Am I too late, Amity?" he asked, chagrined. "I have come to take you to Weston Manor, if you wish it, after your mother has paid her respects to your uncle and aunt."

"Yes, Finlay, I want to go with you." Her feet flew, and suddenly Amity was in his arms, pressed against his chest so hard that the cold metal of his jacket buttons burned her bare skin. His mouth was cold, but when he parted to admit her wholly inappropriate and excessively enthusiastic kiss, she found warmth. Amity felt weightless with joy even after her feet touched the floor again.

"I see." Her mother grinned at her from behind him. "You have had a very successful Christmas visit indeed."

After a frosty reunion between the Mayweather woman who had once ruled Wells House and the present occupants, the sisters bundled back into the sleigh for a final night journey over the snowbound fields to Weston Manor.

Holly, who had dispatched her maid to assist Amity with gathering her few belongings, waved wistfully from beneath the portico, her crimson shawl visible long after she and Finlay swept away over the winter landscape in a second sleigh with her trunk in the front seat next to the driver. Stars twinkled overheat like millions of knowing eyes. Bells on the horses' tack jingled merrily in the dark night. But best of all, Amity was tucked next to Finlay. Contentedness spread through her limbs. Amity yawned.

"Is that where you went for all this time? To Kearny?" she asked in a puff of steam, although she already knew the answer. How else would her mother and sisters have arrived here?

"I realized, Amity, that I have been a poor friend to ever since Ellis...passed." He squeezed her shoulder and turned serious. "I thought it was more than I could bear to see anyone affiliated with your brother—most especially, you. But instead, the opposite happened."

"How do you mean?" asked Amity, bewildered.

"I couldn't understand at first why you disliked me so. Then, I thought, 'why should Amity care for me?'" He swallowed. "I realized I had disappeared from your life when you needed me most. I had no idea what had happened to you, apart from your mother's decision to move the family to a village where..."

"You can say it. Kearny is all charm and no opportunity."

Finlay squeezed her hand. "It occurred to me that your

mother's jointure might have been insufficient to support a family of five women, but no one had ever thought to inquire after your welfare."

"I don't understand why this affects you now." Amity didn't want to ruminate upon the past. Yet, they needed to put this behind them. A future as bright as the stars beckoned.

"My own feelings about returning to my childhood home had been complicated. But my feelings about you, Amity Mayweather, are not." Finn cupped her chin with one gloved hand. Amity had believed there could be no more perfect kiss than the one he had graced her with beneath the mistletoe. She was wrong. This kiss surpassed that by far. When they paused for breath, he whispered, "The moment I fell on you in a snow fort, I knew you were the beacon whose light I had been missing for ages. You fill a hollow ache I can hardly describe. The moment you pledged yourself to another man, I wanted to take revenge."

Finlay's grip tightened fractionally. Amity clutched his forearm and whispered, "I never meant to. I felt sorry for Lunt, and for myself. My attempt to be noble by standing aside while you courted Holly caused more heartache this Christmas than any of my aunt and uncle's cold attempts to play matchmaker. Know this, Finlay Weston. I will fight tooth and nail against anyone who attempts to come between us again. I am honored that you came back for me."

Amity kissed him this time, sliding her gloved hand up the front of his wool coat. They continued this way for the half-hour ride to Weston Manor. By the time they arrived at Weston Manor, the time was well past midnight and the state of their clothing was disreputable. Apart from a sidelong glance as them, Amity's mother said nothing.

"Mary Anne fell asleep," Leticia said the instant the sleighs pulled up to the grand, snow-caked edifice.

Mrs. Mayweather scanned his face. "Can you carry her?"

"Yes." Finlay lifted Mary Anne as though the gangly, nearsighted girl weighed nothing. The six of them trooped into the house expecting emptiness, only to find...

A fire dancing in the parlor grate. The scent of curing plaster, mixed with beeswax from the candles along the hallway, permeated the air.

"The ladies' rooms are ready and waiting," said a bowing bewigged man whom Amity presumed to be the butler. "If I may show you the way."

Finlay carried Mary Anne's inelegantly sleeping form after his servant, taking great care not to knock her head or feet against the wall. Amity exchanged a smile with her mother.

"There are only two guest rooms prepared, sir," explained the butler apologetically, unlocking a freshly stained oak door that swung open on silent hinges. Inside was a large four-poster bed hung with gold-fringed ivory brocade. Amity could smell the freshly hung wallpaper. Mary Anne barely stirred as Finlay laid her gently onto the bed.

"We can manage from here, Mr. Weston," her mother said quietly. Beside her, Charity yawned. "Thank you for brightening our holidays."

"It is a pleasure to reacquaint myself with the family. If I can bring a bit of merriment to my former neighbors at this bleak time of year, I am grateful for it." Finlay bowed.

"I don't know how Amity is to fit in the bed with us," complained Charity. "Your snoring is bad enough, Letty."

"I do not snore," replied Leticia, who absolutely snored in the most unladylike fashion.

Amity tried to suppress a smile, but it took her mouth hostage anyway. "I can sleep in the—"

"In my bedroom," Finlay interjected. "I shall rest on the chaise lounge in the antechamber. I had it moved out of storage for this purpose." He bowed to Mrs. Mayweather. "Amity shall have the key. Her virtue is safe."

Years of careworn toil fell away from her mother's face as she smirked up at Finlay Weston. "If she wants it to be."

"Mother," Amity chided, her cheeks heating. "Finlay and I have much to discuss, as do we. I shall see you in the morning." She kissed her mother's cheek and smelled the comforting scent of rosewater. Amity's throat closed.

"We have all had a long Twelfth night," Finlay said gently. Gently he tugged her

"Thank you, Finn," Amity whispered. She trailed him down the hall, past the foyer.

"It is nothing I ought to have done much sooner," Finlay replied, keeping his hands crossed behind his back. "Amity, I know this is not the proper time to ask you, but my feelings will not be stopped. Will you do me the honor of consenting to be my bride?"

"Finn," Amity whispered into the darkness. Her gloved hand sought and found his as they ambled slowly up the stairs to the second floor and down a hallway cluttered with workmen's tools. Ladders. Buckets. Shadowy objects she couldn't identify. "You know the answer is yes. A thousand times, yes."

"I ask because I know how much you resented your aunt's interference. I do not wish to repeat the same mistake. I have asked your mother's permission. I believe in taking the proper—"

Amity cut him off with a kiss. Her foot connected with a bucket, which tipped and rolled, but Finlay caught her in his arms to lift her against his chest. "You are annoyingly proper at the most inconvenient moments, Finlay Weston."

He grimaced. "Indeed. Had I been a measure less devoted to doing the honorable thing toward your cousin, we might have come to an agreement sooner. I have learned my lesson, however, and I intend to be utterly improper with you for as often as possible."

Amity laughed, and the sound echoed through the empty hall as Finlay fumbled with the door to his chambers. She tumbled onto the crimson bedspread, playing with the embroidered flowers at her bodice.

He tumbled onto the bed beside her, lengthwise across the width of the bed. "In one sense, the Mayweathers have achieved one of their objectives. Their twelve nights of hosting will surely be the talk of many a Hertfordshire Christmas to come." Finlay traced the indent of her waist through too many layers of wool and linen. "Do you want me to retreat to the antechamber, Amity?"

"No, Finn. I wish for you to stay here with me."

He stroked her hair and cupped her cheek. "I have taken the liberty of securing a special license. Should we wish to exercise it."

"You have been busy, Mr. Weston," Amity whispered against his cheek.

He turned to kiss her, open-mouthed. A long moment passed as they explored the contours of one another's bodies, close beside one another in the cold room. Amity unwound his cravat and flipped the buttons of his waistcoat free. She found hard muscles beneath unthinkably soft skin, contrasting with a whorl of rough hair. Delighted, she moved her hand south.

"Amity," he groaned as she teased the hard ridge of his arousal.

"Finn," she whispered against his warm bulk. "Make me yours. Forever."

And he did.

❄

Continue with Holly's swoony Christmas adventure when you read *Twelve Nights of Ruin*, a steamy opposites attract, grumpy/sunshine, marriage of convenience novella.

Twelve Nights of Ruin

BOOK 2

Chapter One

CHRISTMAS, 1817

"The gentleman holding up the fireplace, Holly, is your husband-to-be."

Miss Holly Mayweather's mother gestured to the blunt-featured, broody man whose open palm rested on a corner of the massive carved stone gargoyle's forehead holding up the mantlepiece. He had arrived but a quarter hour ago—unforgivably late for a house party. A faint scent of damp snow emanated from his jacket. Gloves dangled from his free hand as though he had forgotten to pass them over to the valet. The sight of him jolted Holly out of a malaise which had afflicted her ever since the abrupt announcement of her betrothal a fortnight earlier.

"That gargoyle?" Holly quipped. Her mother glared daggers.

"Not the statue. The man."

"I confess I cannot discern any difference," Holly countered, with exaggerated pleading eyes. Even her parents wouldn't be so cruel as to saddle her with such a sullen specimen of husband.

Would they?

In the four years since her coming out she had managed to evade matrimony with enviable success. London's ballrooms were flooded with hollowed-out men like the one gripping that gargoyle's face like he was the last man standing between it and doom. A delicate shudder wracked her. Holly's tastes ran to fine gowns, witty conversation and dancing late into the night—not cosseting wounded soldiers who never spoke about anything but the horrors they had witnessed at war. Holly was not made for endless dreary conversation designed to make her feel ungrateful and foolish for liking nice things and pleasant people. She was made for mirth and merriment, a terrific hostess, an excellent dancer, and a life of ease and joy.

Ever since she had taken London by storm, she had set her sights set upon a better match than a dreary soldier. Specifically, Lord Pickford, a man well above her station who, until very recently, had seemed equally enamored of her.

"Unlike the statue, Holly, Mr. Reynard Sharp established himself first as a spy and later as Wellington's chief strategist in the war against Napoleon," Mrs. Mayweather informed her reverently. "Without Mr. Sharp, many more of our brave young men would have died in battle."

Holly was perfectly cognizant of the man's credentials. Ever since her disgrace three weeks ago, her mother had made sure to remind her daily of how lucky she was to have an offer of marriage, sight unseen, from man favored to receive a knighthood from the Prince Regent himself. Yet his prospects did nothing to offset her discomfort with how Sharp's dark gaze bored through her. She lifted her chin, quirked one brow and cast Mr. Sharp the cool, dismissive glance that she had perfected through her four seasons. Sharp lowered his gaze to his gleaming Hessians. What had become instantly fascinating about a pair of well-maintained boots, Holly could not possibly guess.

What splendid conversations they could look forward to, she mused bitterly. *Do you take sugar?* she might ask over their first afternoon tea. The man might grunt his assent, or his disapproval. Impossible to interpret. She would deposit a lump in his teacup and he would pretend to enjoy it while grimacing at the sweetness. The one topic of possible interest, his wartime exploits, would never be discussed lest it raise unhappy memories for him. Or, worse, he might never shut up talking about them. No woman wanted a husband who banged on about the glory days of his youth, after all.

"What if we don't suit?" Holly asked, not that it would sway her mother one way or the other. Mrs. Mayweather didn't care how her daughter felt about the match.

Her mother's generous mouth puckered into a thin, disapproving line. "What if you do?"

Touché.

"I only mean, Mama, that Mr. Sharp appears to be an unusually dour sort of man. How on earth did you select him for me?" Holly chose her barb and baited the hook well.

Her parents had married in an arranged match after having been introduced as youths during her mother's first season. Their union had proved both fruitful and loving. Naturally, they were firm adherents to the tradition of matchmaking that had brought them so much shared joy. Neither of her parents had been pleased with Holly's approach to flirting her way through London.

Why can't you be more like your cousin, Amity? they would lament, not infrequently. *She is sweet-natured and biddable.*

Until she hadn't been. Much to Holly's relief, last Christmas, Amity had stolen the man her parents had previously selected for Amity's husband right out from everyone's noses. That near miss had made Holly even more determined to land a proposal from Lord Pickford. She quite fancied being called *lady*.

"I cataloged each of Lord Pickford's singular personal qualities and sought out the direct opposite," her mother said repressively.

Cold embarrassment washed through Holly. That explained a great deal about this wretched match. Unfortunately for her, Lord Pickford had a secret that Holly—despite all her carefully cultivated urban polish—had never imagined. A secret that had exploded into view and sent him fleeing to the continent with his *male* lover.

Holly had been shocked to her core to learn that men could engage in physical love that way—although with the wisdom of retrospect, it explained a great deal about his reluctance to propose to her.

For two years, Pickford had implied he would confer upon her the right to be titled *lady* in exchange for a *companionable marriage*. A true sophisticate would have understood the bargain he offered. Holly's embarrassment that she had not understood his terms properly at all curdled her stomach, even now. She had been nothing but a useful fool.

In the end, just a fool.

Holly's sure bet had become her downfall. Mrs. Mayweather's mouth and eyes had acquired a permanently narrow pinch whenever she gazed upon Holly, and she had sworn that by Twelfth Night, Holly would be someone else's problem.

Well, this was only Christmas Eve. Her mother hadn't won yet. She still had time to convince the soldier that she was nothing more than what she appeared to be: a vapid flirt without a serious bone in her body.

The man presently ignoring Holly from not ten feet away did not look like the sort of husband inclined to be indulgent of his wife. Nor was Holly prone to becoming a biddable spouse.

This marriage was going to be a disaster. It must be

stopped. By any means necessary. Once she got back to London for the spring Season, she would find her own substitute and marry him, posthaste. She had an entire coterie of men who had made various promises if only she would do them the honor of becoming their wife. All she had to do was choose one.

Holly bit her lower lip. Mr. Sharp was passably handsome in a brooding, rough sort of way, but in every other sense, he was a massive step down from Pickford. Even a prospective knighthood couldn't make up for the way he jerked his gaze away whenever she glanced his direction.

"I suppose you ought to introduce us," she sighed.

Chapter Two

Miss Holly Mayweather's physical beauty was beyond anything a bastard-born war hero like Rey Sharp had any right to expect in a wife. Finlay Weston, the one friend since arriving in Herefordshire, had led him to understand that she was "quite pretty," a description that had utterly failed to prepare Reynard for the astonishing loveliness of his intended bride.

Blond curls that had escaped her coiffure danced enticingly about her swanlike neck. Blue eyes like summer skies over bloody battlefields peered at him with suspicion. No woman's lips were that rosy without the subtle application of paint, either. The artifice reminded Reynard—not that he needed it—that Miss Holly Mayweather had only consented to become his wife for lack of any other choice. Her long-standing affection for, and expectation of engagement to, Lord Pickford had left all of London's *ton* wondering how much she knew about the man's affections for other men. Her claims of ignorance hadn't convinced anyone.

Miss Mayweather might not be quite ruined, but at

twenty-three, she was nearly on the shelf and had displayed dismayingly poor judge of character.

Being a strategic-minded fellow, Reynard had spied his chance to acquire a higher-quality spouse than he might otherwise have hoped for. Like working an inside connection to put an early bid on a particularly desirable horse, he had asked Weston to put in a word with Miss Mayweather's father. A flurry of letters with her father had sealed the agreement in principle. Dowry, date, and legal contracts had been drawn up and agreed to.

Within hours of delivering the signed papers, Reynard had received an invitation to Lord & Lady Stapleton's annual holiday house party. To receive such an honor signaled his welcome into the large Mayweather clan, for Lord and Lady Stapleton were godparents to Holly, her two sisters, and three brothers. It had all come together with astonishing speed. Thus, here he was, wearing the embroidered red waistcoat his new valet had declared festive but which Reynard thought gaudy and ridiculous.

He had showed up tonight with his special license in hand, ready to proceed.

But suddenly, he was unsure.

Meeting a young lady of good breeding ought to be far less complicated than gaming out Napoleon's next moves on a board, but the emotion that flickered over Miss Mayweather's delicate features rocked him.

Despair.

His stomach tightened as if one of Napoleon's spies had planted a fist in his midsection. How dare she be sad at the prospect of marrying him? He had done nothing to earn her disfavor.

The spoiled beauty clearly didn't want to give him a chance.

He jerked his attention to the fire dancing in the grate.

The flames mocked his hubris in thinking he could snare a beautiful woman into becoming his wife. Acquiescence was a long way from willingness.

Absently, he shifted his weight from his injured leg to the stronger side. He'd healed well. He hadn't lost the use of his limb, like so many had. But for a woman who reputedly enjoyed dancing, his infirmity suddenly felt like an insurmountable flaw.

He became abruptly aware of the moisture gathering at the back of his neck and abruptly moved away from the fire. He'd been standing too close to the roaring blaze, that was all. It was natural for a man to feel some degree of anxiety before changing his life so profoundly.

The mere thought of tying himself to a woman who had every reason to betray him made the taste of sickness rise in the back of his throat. Miss Mayweather did not want him, which begged the question: how long would Holly honor her wedding vows?

Not that he was the sort of man who would deny a child simply because it wasn't his. He was not his father. Rey knew what it was like to grow up without a father and have to make his own way in the world.

He shook his head. His friend, Mr. Finlay Weston, had promised that Miss Mayweather was a reasonable girl. Woman, rather.

From the crown of glossy curls above her perfect forehead to the toes of her boots, there was not a hint of girlishness about her. Especially not the way her breasts filled out the low scoop of her bodice.

Miss Mayweather reacted to his admittedly intrusive examination with brows knit disapprovingly over the bridge of her nose. Hastily, he straightened. Reynard coughed to cover his discomfort at having been caught looking at his future bride's breasts. Then, he immediately worried that the attempted cover had made him appear unwell.

Rey was not accustomed to conversing with fine women. Any women, really. There were the whores who trailed after the army, and the village girls who sometimes fell for one of the men stationed nearby. Not Rey, though. He had suffered through many months of lonely nights while in service to the Crown. Not that he had been a saint, for fuck's sake—

"Mr. Sharp?"

He started. "Miss Mayweather?"

She nodded once, quick and decisive. Blond curls bounced playfully despite her serious expression. "We are to be married tomorrow morning by special license. I thought it best to make some acquaintance prior to entering into such a permanent relationship."

Holly Mayweather's bright determination instantly made Reynard want to equally impress her.

"Only if you wish it," he said quickly. He? Married, to this bold beauty? Impossible. Worry scratched over the back of his neck like caterpillar feet. He swallowed.

"Have I any other options?" she asked. Her brows arched upward in two arcs of surprise. Eyes as light as a clear spring on a summer day regarded him with suspicion and...hurt.

"I don't know," Rey answered honestly. "Do you?"

Her jaw tightened. Small pink spots bloomed over the apples of her cheeks. "If I did, I wouldn't be here, would I? Marrying a complete stranger?"

Rey's mouth welded shut, mercifully, lest he utter any further stupidity. In all his twenty-nine years he had never felt like such a dunce. Holly Mayweather fried his brains the way lighting had once struck an army captain and left him a scramble-minded shadow of his former self. Shyness left him tongue-tied when he most needed to say something—anything—clever.

She sighed. "Let's try to put on a good show of it, though, shall we? For my parents? I have a red sash I can wear to match your waistcoat tomorrow." Two even white teeth dug into the plumpest part of her lower lip. "It doesn't appear that we are destined for a lifetime of happiness."

Miss Mayweather's assessment hit with unimaginable force. His world tilted. The room spun. Rey felt both distantly removed and acutely present. Blood throbbed in his temples. Facing down Napoleon's best spies held little terror when compared to her hopeless resignation.

"No, it does not. Though I hope we might learn to tolerate one another well enough, with time," he said roughly. Hearing himself, Rey would have shaken himself. All his confidence at war, undone by a mere *woman*. A cold sheen of perspiration dampened the back of his neck and the small of his back, but Rey drew up the reserves of his dignity.

What was happiness, anyway?

"Miss Mayweather, I trust we can find enough common ground to establish mutual satisfaction in the years to come."

What he could not say out loud—certainly not within earshot of anyone else—was how thoughts of the many ways in which he would see that Holly was thoroughly satisfied, if only she would give him the chance. Not a quarter-hour in her presence, and Rey already knew he would give his life for a single genuine smile from this woman.

Rey could not think of a more dangerous way to start a marriage than letting an overconfident and sophisticated beauty take his heart hostage. He's spent more than a decade strategizing his way into the upper ranks of the military. He could out-scheme one haughty debutante. Once he had established that he was the master, she'd settle into her role of wife and, eventually, mother. All Rey needed to do was ferret out her deepest fears and desires, then exploit them ruthlessly to get what he wanted most of all. Her fidelity, both in bed and out of it.

Chapter Three

"Reynard Sharp, do you take Holly Mayweather to be your lawfully wedded bride?"

The vicar's double chin wobbled like jellied eel above the white and black band of his cassock. The sight brought on a fresh wave of nausea. At her mother's urging, Holly had managed a few bites of her breakfast. She did not wish to be reacquainted with them on a return trip. She resolved not be sick at her own wedding, no matter how desperately she did not want to marry the stone-faced man at her side.

He would crush her. Not only in bed, with his muscular physique, but in spirit. Ever since screwing up her courage to introduce herself without the benefit of anyone's assistance yesterday afternoon, Holly found herself regretting every twist of fate that had brought her to this moment. But if there was one choice she could take back, it would have been speaking with her husband-to-be. Holly had spent a sleepless night convincing herself that taking a vow of silence was the only way to save her own hide. She might as well join a convent.

The very notion was enough to make her chuckle bleakly.

"No, sir. I am afraid I do not take Miss Mayweather as my lawfully wedded wife."

Holly's ears burned as the deep rumble of her not-husband's voice pounded through her like a canon blast. The longest sentence she had heard him speak in their brief acquaintance, and he *rejected* her?

A gasp from the few people assembled behind them echoed up the beautiful stone archways. Cold. Serious. The Stapleton's private chapel was a perfect symbol for her marriage. There was no space for warmth or affection or, God forbid, love.

"I beg your pardon?" Holly said in a gasp of outrage. If anyone was going to reject this marriage, it was going to be *her*. How *dare* he beat her to the punch?

"I must clarify, sir," Reynard Sharp said to the vicar. Not to her. Of course. Why should he directly address the woman he was essentially abandoning at the altar on Christmas morning? "I mean that I wish to postpone the ceremony until Miss Mayweather and I have had a chance to become better acquainted."

"As though time will help matters." Holly's temper overrode her sense. First Lord Pickford's total abandonment, now Reynard Sharp's last-minute hesitation? What had she done to deserve such humiliation? Dance a few dances? Seek happiness? What was life worth, without happiness?

The man beside her cast her a sidelong glare as cutting as a blade. Hurt tears stung her eyelids. Holly's pride prevented them from doing anything worse than dampening her lashes.

"I would like a week to court my bride." A ghost of a smile touched the corners of his mouth. For a split second, Holly could imagine merriment, even laughter, crinkling the corners of his eyes. The startling thought cut through the haze of her feelings.

He wanted to court her.

Properly.

Not simper platitudes over her proffered hand to make her giggle, as Lord Pickford had done.

Holly swallowed past the knot of emotions in her throat. She had been such a simpleton, believing him a friend. Trusting that if she displayed enough charm, wit and patience that he would eventually love her. Had she paid as much attention to the way young ladies flitted in and out of his orbit as she had to the splendidness of Pickford's waistcoats, Holly might have understood earlier that Pickford's clutch of permanent male friends were not an annoyance. They were his true loves. She had been their unwitting window-dressing. It distressed her immensely every time she thought about it, that not a single one of her supposed friends in London had ever thought to give her warning.

Perhaps she ought to give Reynard Sharp a chance.

"You know what they say, marry in haste, repent at leisure," Holly said brightly. How was it possible that her face froze and burned at the same time? Her mouth was stuck in a stretched half-grimace, half-grin that she hoped did not look half as fearsome as it felt. The vicar shot her a chiding scowl. Holly wished for a hole to open in the cold stone floors and swallow her. But no such relief was forthcoming.

"*Holly*," her mother hissed in reprimand.

"Miss Mayweather is correct." Mr. Sharp's directness caught Holly off-guard. "Marriage is a solemn oath not to be taken lightly. A few days to get to know one another would not be ill-advised."

"Exactly," Holly agreed quickly. A rush of relief threatened the integrity of her posture and knees. Fainting was a real possibility. The vicar, unimpressed with their mutual hesitation, frowned. "With the special license, we can simply adjust the date."

"That isn't how it works," the vicar sputtered.

"Who is to know that the date was changed? We can call this a practice," interjected Mrs. Mayweather, and for once, Holly was grateful for her mother's support.

"Why not proceed with the ceremony and apply for an annulment if the union proves unbearable?" said Mr. Mayweather She winced. Was she such an awful daughter that her own father wished to dispose of her by any means available?

The vicar sighed heavily. "I think, madam, that Mr. Sharp's measured approach is in everyone's best interests."

"Quite right, sir. A few more days cannot make any difference to Holly's tattered reputation. If a few days is all it takes to ensure a happier match, we shall permit Mr. Sharp the liberty to court his wife." Lord Stapleton spoke, and it was decided. Mrs. Mayweather's mouth set into a hard, straight line, but she bowed her head in acquiescence.

"One week," Holly's father declared. "Seven days. Make good use of them. Do not forget the masked ball two evenings hence. Tomorrow, the guests for the house party begin to arrive."

The family began to disperse. Alone, Holly raised her gaze to meet Mr. Sharp's for the first time. "Promise me this. If either of us decides we do not suit, we may back out without consequences."

"I will, if you promise me this in return. Give me a real chance to win your affections."

Startled at his vulnerability, Holly swallowed. True, she had come to this union expecting the worst. Last night, Mr. Sharp had taken her fears and amplified them. They were very different people. Yet there was a thread of…something. She did not know what to call it. Not quite hope, but the possibility of it. A strand of spider's silk when she needed a lifeline. She reached for it anyway. "You have it."

He relaxed fractionally. "My word is my honor, Miss Mayweather. If, at the end of seven days, you do not wish to marry me, I will not force you to go through with the ceremony."

Words clogged her throat, so instead Holly bobbed her chin in terse acknowledgement.

Mr. Sharp captured her hand. He bent his head to kiss the back, like Pickford might have done. Holly snatched it back, stiffening. Mr. Sharp closed off the way he had relaxed a few moments before. With a subtle shift of posture.

Like it or not, she could read his emotions. They echoed her own. Holly did not know what to make of the electric current that vibrated up her arm in the aftermath of their brief contact. It was too much.

Too much disapproval.

Too much desperation.

Too much…everything.

Holly had no reserves. She wanted the comfort of her cousin, Amity, the only person who had ever been her real friend. She would arrive soon, with her husband, Finlay Weston, the man Holly's parents had tried to get her to marry one year ago at Christmas. Until then, all Holly wanted was to be alone.

With a final glance at the man who had tilted her entire world off-center, Holly turned on her heel and strode after her parents. Reynard Sharp's abrupt interest in winning her heart, when he already had her hand, was a balm to her shame-seared soul.

❋

Boxing Day was an event Reynard had only ever experienced from the receiving end.

Castoff goods and, in wealthier households like the Stapleton's, lengths of quality wool for new clothing were distributed to household staff. It was a joyous event celebrated by a feast and a day off. Growing up, Reynard had always been glad when his mother came home for the afternoon with her gifts.

After he was born, she had found a place as head maid with a local family. They were not nearly as wealthy as the last family she had worked for previously, but his mother was relieved to find employment so close to home. As a child he had lived with his grandparents on their small farm. His mother had visited every week until she prevailed upon his father to finally send him away to school at the age of ten. That had lasted for five lonely years. By sixteen, he was back at the smallholding, and at seventeen, he made his final request of his natural father. Four hundred pounds to purchase his commission as an ensign in the army—an unimaginable sum to a poor farm boy.

With the understanding that I shall never hear your name spoken or find your illegible scrawl on my silver salver again, your request is granted, Mr. Sharp. The same goes for the woman who spawned you. Thruppence to a whore would have been a far better investment than this constant bleeding of moneys for a boy who was naught but a mistake.

He'd never forgotten the expression on his mother's face when she showed him the note. "I loved him," she'd whispered, barely audible, with a stricken faraway blankness in her eyes. In that moment he had despised his sire. If Miss Sharp had given him up as an infant and turned him over to a foundling home, she could have retained her good name and perhaps married. His mother might have had other children to love instead of doting on him for one afternoon a week during her time off. But Miss Sharp hadn't hesitated to keep him. She had chosen the hard but loving path.

The bitter lesson Rey had learned was that money and kindness were unrelated. The more of the former one possessed, the less of the latter one displayed.

He vowed to make the most of his father's final gift. By the age of twenty, he had worked his way up to the rank of Captain. For his entire ten years in the service, his mother used a portion of her annual allotment of linen to make him new clothes, just as she had done while he was growing up. He had saved his wages to purchase the next higher commission and courted higher-ranking officers to sponsor his rise. Soon, once he knew for certain that the knighthood and its accompanying living would be his, he would tell her the good news. Until then, it was best to keep it secret. There was no good to be had of getting her hopes up. Rey hadn't even told her that he was getting married, he held so little optimism for the union.

"I expect you'll be the one passing out boxes next year."

The dulcet voice of Miss Mayweather seized him by the ear. Reynard stiffened. He had not heard her come up behind him. How long had she stood nearby as he ruminated over his past? "What makes you say that?"

"I understand you are to receive a knighthood," she said lightly.

"Oh? And does that make you more inclined to accept me as a husband?"

Holly cast him a narrow glare, clearly offended. "I don't know what you mean."

"I have heard you would not marry any man unless he came with a title." Excellent move there, repeating gossip about Miss Mayweather to her face. Reynard wanted to melt into the floor.

"Is that what people say about me?" she mused a little

sadly. "I suppose there's some truth to it. No one ever tells you these things to your face. I find your honesty quite refreshing, Mr. Sharp."

Quite refreshing. Damned with faint praise was a phrase that had been invented for this moment. Miss Mayweather's tongue was as sharp as a rapier. She wielded it with quick slashes that left one bleeding before he knew what had cut him. He must say something, but Rey could summon nothing coherent so all he did was bob his chin.

Miss Mayweather curtsied. Perfectly proper. Deliciously pert. A commotion broke out in the sumptuous tableau of Lord and Lady Stapleton passing out boxes. He bit back a grin as a maid overcome with emotion embraced the dignified Lord Stapleton around the neck. When he glanced back at Holly, he found a bemused smile on her pretty face as well. He could picture them passing out gifts to hard-working servants in a ritual like this one. He planned to be generous —which probably meant Holly would object, given she was born to this miserly class. His optimistic mirage of future joy evaporated.

"Where are your parents?" he asked, after a long moment of silence.

"Presumably performing this same ritual with our tenants. They left yesterday afternoon and will return in the morning."

"You didn't go with them," Reynard observed.

"I thought it would be better for me to remain here. For you to court me, of course. I assume you still intend to do so." Miss Mayweather did not look up at him. Her attention remained focused on the happy display of unboxing taking place in the center of the parlor. Twin pink spots decorated her pale cheeks.

"Of course," he said quickly, reminded that he had no idea of how to go about properly courting a woman. The military had left little time for entertaining well-bred ladies. Asking her to dance was, obviously, out of the question. Asking to call upon her was unnecessary considering they were both temporarily in residence beneath the Stapleton's capacious roof. "Have you had an opportunity to visit the library?"

Earlier, Reynard had taken a peek into the well-stocked library with rows of morocco-bound volumes stacked neatly into dark wood shelves. This, to him, was luxury. An inner sanctum of history, intelligence and refinement the likes of which—had his father done the right thing by his mother—Rey might have had access to much earlier in life. Upon finding him in the doorway, kindly Lord Stapleton had clapped him on the shoulder and invited him to explore the collection at his leisure. A child invited to raid a confectioner's shop could not have been more delighted.

It was therefore to his great embarrassment that Holly's nose wrinkled ever so slightly right beneath the inner corners of her eyes. An elegant gesture that whispered of deep disapproval, the way a lady might indicate she had detected the distinct odor of flatulence and suspected you to be the source. But almost as soon as her disappointment had scratched his ego, Holly beamed up at him with wide smile and parted lips, between which he glimpsed her even white teeth.

"I should love to see the library," she declared. Rey could almost believe she meant it. "Let's go."

"Now?" he asked with astonishment.

Holly Mayweather casually looped her arm through his elbow. "No time like the present," she said, steering him away from the gifting. Her touch made a lump form in his throat. With cold shock, Reynard felt the uncomfortable rise of a second lump growing in his trousers. This was surely not the way to court a fine lady.

"Did you like working for Wellington?" Holly asked as they wandered, arm-in-arm, down twisting, empty hallways.

What did she mean, precisely? "As in, did I enjoy the experience?"

Holly laughed. Not the artificial tinkling sounds that fine ladies often made, but a true giggle, charming and light-hearted. "Isn't that what 'like' usually implies?"

"You ask difficult questions, Miss Mayweather."

"Holly. My given name is Holly. I invite you to use it." She squeezed his forearm and winked up at him. Reynard's lungs felt inadequate to the task of drawing breath. Was she… flirting with him?

"Rey," he gasped, coughing slightly to cover his discomfort. He had endured his share of adolescent attractions to the opposite sex, but never had he been so besotted as to forget his own name. "My friends call me Rey."

"It's a pleasure to make your acquaintance, Rey," Holly declared lightly. She cast him another sidelong grin, as though they had a shared secret. When she wasn't being caustically sarcastic, she could make you feel like the center of her world. He wondered how half of London had avoided falling in love with her. Perhaps, the men had, but she'd spurned them in favor of titled gentlemen.

"Likewise." They fell into a comfortable stride, he shortening his to match her light steps. "To answer your question, I very much enjoyed working with the man."

He considered this a satisfactory answer. Holly, however, remained curious.

"What did you like about working with him?" she prompted.

"He was the coolest head I have ever seen under fire, for one thing." Reynard paused, searching for the right words. "I suppose he would have to be, considering the amount of death he had seen and ordered in his many years in the military."

Still, this was not enough.

"How did you meet him?" Holly asked.

"Do you always ask so many questions?"

"I'm just making conversation. Trying to understand you. Go ahead and ask me something. Anything."

Ah. Her determined cheer was an act. Another artifice—and he had fallen for it. "Why didn't Lord Pickford marry you?"

Holly stumbled. Her fingers, which had been loosely tucked into his elbow, dug into his muscle with surprising—and painful—force. Reynard cursed himself and braced her upright. They continued walking as though nothing had happened. A long moment of silence passed.

"Because he was in love with men," she said softly. Her hand slipped away from his arm. A few inches of distance opened between them.

"Were you shocked to find out?" Reynard had heard the relevant facts of the scandal, of course. He was aware of such proclivities from his time in the military. No matter how harsh the punishment, some men were simply made to love other men. He had long ago accepted that as God's will and undeserving of human disdain.

"Yes, and no," she said with a pensive crease to her brow. Thoughtful Holly appealed even more to him than flirtatious Holly. Hers was a face fashioned for mirth and fun. Seriousness did not suit her.

They could not be more diametrically opposed.

Yet, perhaps there was hope for happiness if they could meet halfway between frivolity and earnestness. When they arrived at the library there was no one inside. They had the room to themselves.

"Now that we may speak freely..." Holly squared her

shoulders. She did not glance at the volumes lining the walls of the hushed room. "I knew, vaguely, that sometimes men prefer men's company to women's. I didn't think..." Holly pressed her fist against her mouth.

Oh, no. Not that. Anything but tears.

To Rey's great relief, she did not cry. With a great exhale, she said, "Pickford enjoyed my company, and I his. It therefore never occurred to me that company could also be a euphemism for..." A deep blush broke over her cheeks. "Physical relations. Not that I know anything about them, of course."

"Of course," Rey repeated woodenly. "I never would have conjectured so." He felt utterly helpless in the face of Holly's distress and his own embarrassment. He had not been prepared for her forthrightness. Perhaps he had been too quick to write her off as frivolous.

"What I mean to say is that I know what they are. I am not ignorant. I will not...disappoint you." Holly cleared her throat. "On our wedding night, I mean. I promise to be subservient. Obedient."

His abdomen clutched in horror. As though he wanted any of those things from her. No, Reynard wanted her inquisitiveness and bright personality, the way she had been with him this afternoon. Her acceptance of Pickford's lovers had taken him off-guard. There was much more to Holly Mayweather than pretty dresses. Although words escaped him, he dared to bridge the distance between them and cup her cheek in his palm. A man could drown in the blue depths of her gaze.

He refused to do that. Holly Mayweather might have made a habit of wrapping men around her delicate little pinkie finger, but she would not succeed with him. Reynard would tame her, break her to bridle like an untrained filly. Never cruelly. He was a military man and not above such tactics, but as Wellington had taught him, they were most effective when used sparingly. He resolved never to break Holly's bright spirit—and also not to dance before it like a moth to a candle.

"I don't want subservient," he said roughly. Her lower lip was silk beneath the pad of his thumb. Holly's eyes darkened. The tip of her tongue touched him. An electric frisson made his abdomen clench. One taste would do. For now. "On our wedding night, Holly, I want all your unfeigned passion. I'll accept nothing less than raw honesty from you."

She jerked her head away. Shaken by the depth of his own feelings, Reynard pulled back. His hand trembled as he ran it through his hair.

"Fortunately for you, Mr. Sharp, raw honesty is my singular talent," Holly said after a moment. There was a tremor in her voice that belied her confident words. Beneath them, he heard notes of uncertainty and giddy expectation. Her emotions mirrored his own. Still, if she hadn't half-turned to peek back at him over her shoulder in the most outrageously flirtatious gesture he had ever seen, there was no way Reynard would have ever done what he did next.

He strode after her, pulled her into his arms and... kissed her.

Chapter Four

This was no gentlemanly peck on the cheek. Nor was it a furtive buss of closed lips against chastely, firmly sealed ones. No, this was a claiming, and Holly relished it.

Rey's arm found the indentation of her waist. He clasped her body hard against his firm chest. Her hands found the fine wool of his lapels and crept up...and up, until they wound around his neck. The crisp texture of his hair shocked her clear to her toes. And the first taste of his kiss undid her. Rey slanted his mouth over hers and delved his tongue inside, testing. Taking. She opened to him. Her fingers curled against the nape of his neck as she tried to pull him closer. She was on tiptoe, stretching to meet him, wanting more. Holly had been waiting for this moment her whole life. The one kiss of true love. How lucky for her that it was with her husband-to-be.

They were so absorbed in their embrace that neither of them registered the smooth opening of the library doors until a shaft of light cut across their faces.

"In here is the library which you are welcome to...Oh."

Lord Stapleton stood in the opening flanked by newly arrived guests Holly didn't recognize. Rey's body stiffened and he withdrew his arms from her waist. Ice water flashed through her veins. Holly had to remind herself that there was no scandal in an engaged couple enjoying a kiss—a public engagement was as good as binding. Had they gone through with the ceremony yesterday, they would already have been married. But they weren't, and so technically this was improper.

What rot. No woman had ever gotten with child from a kiss—Holly at least knew that much. Although, if such a thing were possible, Holly would definitely be pregnant now.

No matter. In a week they'd be wed. To her immense satisfaction, Rey appeared profoundly out of sorts. His hair was disheveled and his cravat askew, and if she was not mistaken from the furtive glance she stole in the direction of his trousers, there were the beginnings of male arousal. Lord Pickford had certainly never reacted like that to a kiss.

"Shall I leave you to continue your, erm, conversation in private?" Her godfather winked and tried to close the door. Behind him, the new guests smirked. Holly cast them a saucy wink.

"No, Lord Stapleton, we are finished." Holly didn't give Rey a chance to contradict her. She could spend the next few days angling for a bit more autonomy—more pin money, a certain amount of time spent in her favorite town—and more kisses. Lots and lots of kisses. "Has my cousin arrived yet? Mr. and Mrs. Weston?"

"Yes, a quarter-hour ago. They will be upstairs. Go on, I know how close you are." Lord Stapleton gave her a pat on the cheek. Holly bustled out of the room, quite pleased with herself and how her husband's courtship had gone thus far.

❋

Rey watched Holly scurry out of the library feeling as though his entire world had tilted on its axis. His pulse leapt when she blew him a kiss over her shoulder, but the instant she was out of sight, doubt settled back in like a flock of startled chickens clumsily roosting in his head. Where had she learned to kiss like a courtesan? How could he be so besotted with a woman he scarcely knew? She didn't even like books! Had there ever been a woman as unimpressed by literature as Holly Mayweather?

Reynard squirmed as his disappointed manhood accepted that there would be no coupling tonight. In the meantime, his brain whirled with reasons not to let Holly get the upper hand. It was as though he couldn't turn off the part of him that had been trained and honed to spot an enemy's weakness and exploit it. Except that Holly was not an enemy. She was soft and yielding with all the excitement of a curious maiden. It left him wrestling with a strange mixture of hot and cold roiling his gut. On the one hand, it was natural for a woman of twenty-three to have desire for her husband. It was welcome and not at all inappropriate. So why did it make him feel as if he couldn't trust her?

The problem, he decided, after scanning the shelves and blindly flipping through the pages of a tome on Socrates, was that he wanted to feel in control. Holly's enthusiasm made him feel more like clinging to the neck of a galloping steed into battle. He might be capable of it, but on the occasions he'd had need to, he'd never enjoyed the experience.

A sigh gusted out of him. Perhaps their union wasn't totally hopeless if they stuck to kissing. More likely, he was overthinking the matter. All marriage meant for a man, after all, was that one pledged to honor a woman in body and soul for the rest of his natural life. Had he truly come so close to blindly throwing himself into a union without any opportunity to assess her first? A first-rate pedigree was no predictor of compatibility—

"There you are. Lord Stapleton said I'd find you here."

Reynard's jerked out of his thoughts, where he had become lost in the tangle of insecurities yet again. "Weston. Yours is a most welcome face." He bowed slightly. Finlay Weston's dark head bobbed fractionally in return. A knowing grin overtook his features.

"So, are you a married man yet?" Reynard coughed. The book snapped closed. He startled at the sound which conjured faded memories of gunshots. "I take it that means you haven't made an honest woman out of my wife's cousin yet?" Weston asked sympathetically.

"No," Reynard replied. "I could use a second opinion, Weston. If you don't mind a chat, man-to-man."

"Any time," Weston replied cheerfully. He sauntered over to the brandy decanter displayed prominently on a side table and poured two fingers for each of them. They relaxed into butter-soft dark leather. "Holly Mayweather is quite a handful." He was unsuccessful at concealing a knowing smirk.

Don't think about her breasts. Twin plump mounds formed in his imagination. She was more than handful in bed, and out of it. "She is very beautiful," Reynard mumbled.

"That she is."

"Why didn't you marry her?"

Weston swirled his drink thoughtfully. "Beauty is only part of the equation, Rey. Amity made me feel as though I had come home. Wherever she goes in the world I want to be with her. I suppose I sound like a besotted newlywed in saying so, but as I told you before, choosing Amity had nothing to do with disliking Holly. She is a very desirable bride. It's only…"

He paused.

"Go on," Rey prompted.

"Holly didn't seem ready to settle into marriage. I cannot imagine keeping a lively, intelligent, very social woman cooped up in the country. I doubt a taste of scandal has dampened her spirits. If so, it would be a loss to the world."

"Her parents regard their daughter as an empty-headed flirt." It was a mean thing to say, but in this quiet sanctum Rey had the freedom to speak the truth. "Is she?"

"No, although Holly plays one very well." Weston sipped his brandy. "If she were as stupid as they imply—and having been in your position a year ago, I know exactly how her parents act toward her—Holly wouldn't have been half so successful at outmaneuvering their many attempts to marry her off. No, she is very quick to comprehend people's motivations, probably because she has had so much practice with outwitting her parents at home."

Reynard sat with that for a moment while he finished his brandy. The Mayweathers were uncompromising in what they wanted—namely, Holly married. Yet despite this, they had declined to sweeten her already-generous dowry of five thousand pounds. Reynard had not pressed the matter because he was new to this game of marriage negotiations and had no father to guide him through the delicate task of asking. He now wondered if he had left money on the table. Perhaps he oughtn't be so judgmental about wealthy people and their lack of kindness in relation to the amount of money in their coffers. Besides, there would be no dowry at all if the marriage did not take place. They might sue for breach of promise if he refused to go through with the wedding again. That stunt would not work a second time.

"It will be interesting to see her costume at the masked ball tomorrow," Weston mused into the silence.

"About that. What's a gent supposed to wear?" He suspected that the irony of dressing up as a gentleman would be lost on the majority of Stapleton's guests. To his surprise, Finn granted him the freedom to do exactly that.

"A domino will suffice."

Reynard blanked. "Where am I supposed to obtain one?"

His friend laughed. "Did you not think to bring one?"

"I had more pressing matters on my mind."

"True enough. Come, I'm sure we can either borrow one or ask my valet to improvise with a silk cravat. Stapleton will likely have a few extra." They left their cups in the library for the maids to retrieve. "I can't wait to see what Amity comes dressed as. Holly is supposed to surprise her. I expect it will be something daring enough to give me a heart attack."

❈

"Holly! I am delighted to see you again!" squealed Amity Weston, Holly's cousin and closest friend.

"Not nearly as happy as I am." Holly rushed into her cousin's open arms. The top of her head came to Amity's ear. Less than a month had passed since they had seen one another, yet she was surprised by how easily her arms encircled Amity's lean waist. Holly's branch of the Mayweathers had inherited the family fortune after Amity's father, Holly's uncle, had died. Their mothers did not get along, so Amity's mother and her sisters had decamped to a tiny cottage in a rural town far from the luxury the girls had grown up with. The deprivation had made an indelible mark on her cousin.

"Shall I call you Mrs. Sharp, now?" Amity teased. She held her by the hands. Holly's body tensed, and her cousin's face fell. "What's wrong? Aren't you married?"

"Not yet," she mumbled. To her great horror, tears stung the insides of her eyelids. Holly blinked and forced a smile. "But soon. He wanted us to get to know one another a little better."

"Oh," Amity said, clearly taken aback. "I see."

"We shall be married within the week," she said brightly, as if her heart wasn't picking up pace with every word. "Why don't you get settled in so we can discuss more privately?"

A half-hour later they were ensconced in Holly's room. She had had to evict her younger sister, who grumpily agreed to go in search of the rest of the Mayweather cousins.

"How are you holding up, really?" Amity asked the instant the door closed. "I was so worried about you after the great Pickford scandal."

Holly snorted. "I am as well as can be expected. I swear I had no idea he preferred men."

Amity regarded her with solemn blue eyes just like her own, a family trait. "Even I find it difficult to believe that you weren't aware."

"Well, I wasn't. I was as shocked as anyone."

"I didn't even know men could love other men that way until Finlay pointed out the way his admirers flocked to his side. Of course, I thought you knew. You have always been ten times more sophisticated about these matters than I am."

She and Amity had spent three months, from late September through early December, in London together. Finn had given his new wife a proper season, and Holly had been delighted to show her friends around town. Balls, theatre, musicales, and all the attendant gossip had been given new life by seeing them through her cousin's eyes. Yet there remained a lingering tension between Holly and her former fiancé. Holly's social instincts were too keen to miss the subtle way Finn looked down on her by dismissing the connections she sought to make between the newlyweds and her aristocratic friends.

Holly tried not to take it as rejection. Still, there had been moments when she felt a mild sting. She had reminded herself that she was the interloper in their marriage. Holly had reminded herself that there was little at stake. They did not wish to ingratiate themselves with the aristocratic class, and that was fine.

Then, disaster had struck. Amity and Finn had already returned to their estate in Herefordshire when the news of Pickford's peccadillo had broken. Holly had been left to face her parents' wrath, alone.

"I wish you'd been there," Holly said wistfully, settling back against the pillows. "I could have used a friend."

"We did what we could," Amity said reassuringly. She laid on her side and propped her head on one hand. "Finn met Mr. Sharp in London, briefly, and we invited him to stay with us for the holidays. He has only his mother who lives in reduced circumstances, too far away to visit easily."

Of course, her cousin had a soft spot for a man like Reynard Sharp. Her mother had fallen into reduced circumstances, too. "Are you certain his mother started from circumstances once could reduce?"

Amity's eyes narrowed. "How do you mean?"

"My father told me she was a servant in Mr. Sharp's father's house." She licked her lips, not liking the hardness in her cousin's eyes. "I don't care about that. I did agree to the marriage, after all."

"But you wanted an earl," Amity replied flatly.

"Of course. Given the choice, wouldn't you do the same?"

"Not necessarily. I would evaluate the men as individuals, not by their relative social distinction." Amity pushed herself upright. "I am not swayed by titles."

"Money certainly appealed to you, though," Holly snapped. It hurt to be judged harshly by her favorite person in the world. "Otherwise, you might have married Lunt. Or Tillet. But no, only the richest man at my parents' house party would do for poor Amity Mayweather."

Amity's pale face turned a ghostly shade of white. "How

dare you imply I chose Finn for anything other than his personal qualities."

"Oh, don't be so offended," Holly rolled her eyes in frustration. "All I am saying is that his personal qualities included a substantial fortune. Anyone could see you had feelings for one another. But would the attraction have been quite as strong if he had been a mere parson with a hundred pounds a year living?"

Amity glanced down, but said nothing.

"We all choose our husbands with status in mind. I liked Lord Pickford very much. I believed myself in love with him, and he with me. My parents would have been ecstatic to have an earl for a son-in-law." Holly inhaled a deep breath. "I cannot make all of you happy. I can marry for love, or I can marry for money, or for status. It seems impossible to have all three."

"It isn't," Amity said quickly. "You're right, Holly, I did marry for all three reasons, although love was foremost. I shouldn't judge you for weighing status more. Neither of us are free to choose without such considerations."

Mollified, Holly resumed her place on the bed. "I thought I loved Lord Pickford. It hurts to know he never felt the same."

"I wish he had been honest with you." Amity had tucked her long, slim body into the hard-backed chair next to the fireplace. "After a few conversations with Rey, I thought he would be a good match for you. It was Finn and I who suggested he approach your father. We assured him you were everything he could want in a bride."

"Which meant what, precisely?" After the way her friend had described her to her face, Holly wanted to know exactly how she had been presented to her husband-to-be.

"Loyal, comely, intelligent, affectionate—are you seeking

compliments?" Amity teased, but there was a tightness at the corner of her eyes that made the attempt fall flat.

"I am loyal and affectionate to *you*, Cousin. Not to everyone. Believe it or not, I am discriminating in who I choose to bestow my affections upon." She smiled to soften her words. Right now, she needed her friend's steady warmth, but all she was getting was another dose of skepticism. Holly refused to believe she deserved this degree of universal condemnation. "And to be frank, I am not prepared to bestow my heart upon Mr. Sharp."

Amity raised one hand, palm out, to stop her from speaking.

"I realize he isn't like the men you typically prefer" — meaning Pickford, naturally— "but please give him a chance. Rey is a good man. Hardworking, intelligent, kind. His steady demeanor might complement your…"

"High spirits?" Holly supplied when Amity hesitated.

"Boisterousness," Amity said carefully. "You are intellectual equals, if only you chose more serious pursuits than dancing and gossip. I trust you won't take offense when I say you are much like your mother in the way you follow gossip. Especially when it comes to whom is marrying who."

"Well, I am, in fact, offended." Not much, but a bit. "Women's selection of husband determines the shape of our life for years to come. Is it not wise to consider every possible outcome before making a decision?"

"Yes, but you approach matters as though they are all a game!" Amity exclaimed. "Is it so much to ask that you take a bit more care in choosing one's partner?"

For once, Holly's quick tongue failed her. Several responses crowded into her mind. "What makes you think I don't care? I do not think this a game!"

"I am not criticizing, Holly, but I did watch you flirt your way through every ballroom in London for three months."

"Not every ballroom, I have more discernment than that," Holly snapped. Her companion rolled her eyes and blew a gusting sigh.

"Please, let's not fight. The minute I met him, Holly, I knew Mr. Sharp would be good for you. Please, give him a chance. He is kind, if a bit reserved, and will be devoted to any woman fortunate enough to become his wife."

She let her gaze drop to the counterpane where she picked at a piece of linen. "For you, Amity, I will try to like him. Your good opinion raises him greatly in my estimation. Besides which, I have already agreed to marry him."

Relieved, Amity scooted off the bed. "I want you both to be happy, that's all. Now, will you show me the costumes you had made for us for the masquerade ball tomorrow evening?"

Chapter Five

The next evening...

"Thank you so very much for exchanging costumes with me," Amity Weston, Holly's cousin and closest friend, clasped Holly's gloved hand. "I know you think I'm silly, but I couldn't wear a costume so risqué. Not even to a masquerade ball. I don't have your daring."

"Amity. You stole the man I was intended to marry right out from beneath my nose," Holly teased. Or rather, it was supposed to be teasing. Lately, it seemed as if every single thing she said came out wrong. Holly clasped her friend by the hands. "I am joking. Can you even imagine me, married to Finlay Weston?"

"I am very happy with Finn for my husband," Amity replied, clearly hurt.

"I know you are, because he is perfect for you. Which only goes to show what terrible judges of character my parents are." She pasted a determined grin on her face. Her cousin returned an uncertain, yet hopeful, version of Holly's smile.

"True. Were it up to them, my name now would be Mrs. Amity Lunt. Or possibly Mrs. Amity Tillett."

"Worse," Holly declared, squeezing her friend's hands hard enough that she realized with a shock that she was desperate to maintain a physical connection with the one person in the room who loved Holly unconditionally. "You could have been Mrs. Ames." Mr. Ames had been Amity's prospective suitor at her parents' house party last Christmas until he had displayed a temper that Holly would not want directed toward any woman. Holly shuddered at the notion that any lady's prospects could be so grim as to choose him.

Amity cast her a wan smile. "Are you certain you don't mind? It was natural that we should fall in love, given his friendship with my brother. I would never have stolen your beau for any other reason."

Holly gave another squeeze, lighter this time. "You cannot steal what I don't own. You'll do splendidly tonight. Now, let's go find your husband and let him dance with his Aphrodite."

If only she hadn't been so opposed to marrying a year ago, Holly could have been the one standing proud as Mrs. Weston. Before her marriage, no one with discernment would have called Amity beautiful. Yet, her marriage to Finlay Weston had brought a glow to her cheeks and eased the tense lines of worry that had marred her pretty eyes and lovely mouth. Garbed in a billowy white gown with two gold clasps at each shoulder, a gold belt accentuating her slim waist, and gold jewelry glittering at her wrists and ears, Amity was a vision worthy of the finest ballrooms.

Holly sighed, half-envious, half-gratified. On one hand, she was thrilled to see her favorite person in the world happy. On the other hand, she could help but wistfully wonder what might have been if she had curbed her pride last Christmas and married the man her parents had initially chosen for her.

He would never have made you happy, her heart whispered.

Certainly not the way he and Amity were happy, but, then

again, Lord Pickford hadn't made her any happier. In fact, he had done her material harm. Was it really too much to ask that he inform her he had no intention of offering marriage? Or give her a hint that if he were to have done so, it would be on terms she could never accept? The real betrayal was that he hadn't trusted her enough with his secret. Lord Pickford had used her as a fig leaf for his own respectability. She understood why, and she liked to think she would have gone along with the scheme if he had simply been open with her, but she couldn't forgive herself for playing the fool. He'd known what she desired, and he had teasingly dangled the prospect of an offer before her like a kitten with a string.

Shame was not a feeling Holly was willing to indulge for long, though. She pushed it aside and let Amity lead her through the crowd in search of her husband. They found Finn on a small balcony overlooking the ballroom. Beside him loomed Rey Sharp. Both men wore dominos covering half their faces from nose to eyebrows. Even with their plain evening wear, Holly's body reacted instantly. Heat flushed over her cheeks and chest—her very *exposed* chest. The costume which had seemed so clever weeks ago in London, when she had asked her dressmaker to turn her into Aphrodite and her cousin into Minerva, now felt entirely wrong.

Holly tried to twitch her skirt down over her knees. No wonder Amity had been uncomfortable. The short dress was daring by town standards. Amity stood a few inches taller— on her, it would have been downright scandalous. Holly sighed at her own thoughtlessness. This newfound awareness of her flaws felt as uncomfortable as when her stockings sagged and wrinkled inside her shoe while dancing. No way to fix it; impossible to ignore.

Finlay Weston's gazed skimmed past her, indifferent, until he locked onto his wife's form and brightened like dawn over

London's rooftops. Holly had seen her fair share of dawns after a night out. The soft radiance in his gaze outshone them all.

Contrast that with the way Rey's expression dimmed at the sight of her nearly-naked body. This might be a masquerade, but there was no disguising his disapproval. Awareness tugged at her no matter how she studiously attempted to ignore the way Sharp's attention fell across her body and lingered on her bosom.

Tonight's dance gave Holly an exquisite opportunity to get to know her future husband on a more intimate level. They'd be married by Twelfth Night if it cost Holly every ounce of her dignity. Lord Pickford was not going to ruin her future. She refused to give up home for some measure of happiness between them—especially after the kiss they'd shared yesterday.

His gaze fastened on the dip of her bodice where two plump mounds of her breasts protruded over the silver corset. It was supposed to resemble armor, but Holly didn't feel the least bit shielded from Rey's hungry gaze. When they locked eyes, Holly raised one eyebrow defiantly.

I know what you're looking at, she thought silently. Curiously, she liked it—until Rey jerked his gaze away. His entire body stiffened. For the span of one breath Holly had felt desirable. Wanted. But her betrothed's reaction left her feeling shamed. Maybe she could teach this man to enjoy society, but the greater likelihood was that he would keep her cooped up in the country with nothing in the way of stimulation but producing babies—thus far, he had displayed a healthy interest in all things related to producing children, but Holly wanted more out of life than to devote herself solely to motherhood.

"Rey might care to dance, if you asked him, Holly." Finlay jerked his head at his friend.

"I would not." Rey's eyes tightened at the corners.

"Why?" she demanded. It pulled her stomach into a knot of anxiety. Ever since her arrival, not a single thing she said had come out right. Was there a spark of interest from her future husband, or was she fooling herself?

A muscle in Rey Sharp's jaw moved. "I don't know how to."

"You can't dance," Holly repeated in exasperation. "Again, I ask, why? You have two working legs."

This time, it was the corner of his mouth which tightened into a…smile? Or a grimace? Holly couldn't be certain.

"It's not as if spying for Wellington left much time for learning to waltz," Finlay interjected.

"But reels and quadrilles are commonly taught. Anyone who attended a fair as a child ought to know the basics." It wasn't as if arguing was going to solve anything, but Holly couldn't stop herself. She needed to know whether it was her person Rey objected to, or something else. If it was her person, why had he offered marriage?

Because you're a better bride than a soldier with a fortune and acknowledgment from the crown could otherwise acquire.

Holly was the dented pewter tankard at the local smith's shop. Usable, not unattractive from a certain angle, but a bargain because flawed. She inhaled sharply. A gentle press of Amity's hand at her shoulder helped Holly breathe through it.

"I will dance with you, my lady," Rey said quietly, "when I know I will not disgrace you." He bowed in a perfunctory manner.

You could never disgrace me. The words floated into Holly's mind as though inscribed with an invisible quill. *Not as much as I have already disgraced myself.* A warmth like hope washed through her. Holly wanted to be worthy of this man. She wanted to catch the spark of attraction between them and see where it led. Because she had never in her twenty-three years met a man who interested her more than Reynard Sharp.

※

What to make of Miss Mayweather's costume? Rey would have put money on her dressing as Aphrodite, not Minerva. He was mixing Roman and Greek mythology, probably, but he was not educated in fancy schools and his understanding of history was hardly rote. Despite this Rey recognized the large glittering owl pin fastening one shoulder of her risqué costume. The spear at her left shoulder confirmed it. Fluffs of sheer white fabric puffed over the top of her ivory and silver bodice. More billows spilled out the bottom in a cloud-puff over the tops of her thighs.

Pity, that, for beneath the hem of her scandalously short skirt were two gorgeous calves wrapped in silk stockings and gladiator-style laced shoes. Rey's cravat tried to choke him at the sight. He could easily imagine those trim ankles wrapped around his waist while her sharp heels dug into the small of his back as he pounded—

Not here, man. Not here.

"Please," she said, batting her eyelashes at him. A crystal diadem with a silver owl adorned her brow.

"Not yet." A man had to have his pride, and Holly was tearing his to shreds. He leaned low to murmur in her ear, "I daresay your frock endangers my ability to perform."

Holly's cheeks flushed. Apparently, the easiest way to parry his fiancée was pure honesty. A faint smile tried to sneak across his face. If there weren't so much at stake, and it was only the two of them without this infernal castle party with myriad strangers, they might actually get along. Yet here they were, and Holly undoubtedly liked an audience.

"Perhaps you need to practice first with a less enticing lady." She indicated a shepherdess in a ridiculous blue dress no real shepherdess would ever wear, and a towering wig. A live lamb on a lead festooned with bells and ribbons bleated in confusion. "Perhaps Miss Bo Peep is more to your taste."

"Are you joking, madam." Had he not been the butt of her jest, it would have been genuinely funny.

"I am entirely serious."

It was Finlay who pushed him over the edge. "Go on," he smirked. "Have a bit of fun."

"I'd offer to hold her lamb, except that Finn and I are about to take a turn," Amity said apologetically.

"I'm sure that if Holly can manage a few suitors, she can also manage a confused farm animal for a few moments. After all, there isn't much difference between a pig and a lamb."

Holly's plump, pink lips parted in shock. His slight had landed in the center of Miss Mayweather's pride—a direct hit. So why didn't he feel more satisfaction at finding her weakness and exploiting it? Rey had trained to do precisely that. Yet as he approached the hapless Bo Peep, Rey swallowed and glanced back at his bride-to-be.

"Would you care to dance?" he asked, hoping she would say no. Peep glanced down at the animal straining to escape her side.

"I shall need to find something to do with her," Bo Peep said tentatively.

He was an idiot. A thoroughly besotted, utterly absurd idiot. He glanced back at his friends, wondering why he'd challenged Holly like this. To prove a point? He could not have picked a more asinine way to demonstrate that she did not influence his actions if he'd tried. Hell, he'd gone and proven the opposite.

Wait a minute...where had she gone? Rey had lost sight

of his Minerva. She was no longer on the balcony where he had left her. To Bo Peep's consternation, he scanned the room in search of the woman he had abandoned moments before. The irony was not lost on him. Annoyance speared his midsection at the sight of a Lothario with ostrich feathers towering from his cap now bending over Holly's hand. With a determined grin, Rey's future wife accepted and glided onto the dance floor. A possessiveness he had never before experienced tightened his grip on his dance partner's hand. Gamely, she pretended to go along with his act of kissing his way up her arm and ogling the spectacular bosom that by rights only belonged to him. Well, and to its owner, of course.

"Ow!" She complained, and cast him a narrow glare.

"My apologies," Rey mumbled, feeling oafish. A vaguely familiar female shape overshadowed by a large crown resembling the sun stood nearby. "Excuse me, madam, will you watch the lamb?"

He had to get out there and save Holly from Lothario.

"We can wait for the next dance, my card is not full," Bo Peep protested.

"If you please, madam." He all but shoved the shepherdess into line. He kept his focus on the lady at his side for a strained thirty seconds before his gaze darted back to Holly. He would not be envious, he refused to give way to the sense of inadequacy crawling through his body—

His foot landed on a small, soft lump. Rey's partner winced. "Sorry," he muttered.

"Rey I survive this cotillion with all my fingers and toes intact, Mr. Sharp?" Bo Peep said repressively.

Clearly, he could make her no promises. "Would you like to stop?" he offered, chagrined by his own behavior.

"In the middle of a dance?" Bo Peep sniffed. "It isn't done. Not even at a masquerade."

But Rey's attention had already been drawn back to Holly and her Lothario. She threw her head back and laughed as though she was having the time of her life. It was yet another dent in his armor. Soon, he'd be begging Holly to be his wife —and where would that get him? Passing along his hard-won knighthood and legacy to a bastard child. All because he could not resist a woman who didn't want him.

Or…did she? Holly's arms were stiff at the elbows as if she were trying to hold her partner at bay. On second glance, her smile was fixed in a rictus of determination. When they met his for a split second, fear and anger flashed in her blue eyes.

His woman was in trouble. Rey dropped his grip on Bo Peep and leapt out of the way of the oncoming couple. On instinct, Rey pivoted on the ball of one-foot, tripped Lothario from behind, and twirled the ostrich-feathered man into a shocked shepherdess's arms. Before he could draw breath enough to process the magnitude of what he had just done, Rey bowed to Holly. "If I may have the honor?"

Red spots bloomed over the apples of her cheeks. Minerva, blushing, for him. The couple behind them in the cotillion circle paused. It felt as though the entire room waited with bated breath. But it was probably just him and his insecurities.

"Yes," Holly said in a voice barely above a whisper. Then she was in his arms and they were in motion, their bodies moving as one. In all his years as a soldier, Rey had never felt like as much of a hero as he did in that moment.

Chapter Six

Rey Sharp was not a terrible dancer after all. Relief cut through the tense ball of frustration at her core. Holly had dealt—effectively, thank you very much—with all manner of handsy men. Lothario hadn't posed any real threat. A few too many drinks, a bit too much enthusiasm for the character he had dressed as, and she had played along at the start. Then, he had taken things too far and ignored her increasingly obvious signals of distress. Holly had been one step short of slapping him when her fiancé had intervened.

"Does this happen to you often?" Rey asked.

"No." Holly paused. "I wonder if my recent troubles with Lord Pickford made me seem like…well. A target." He stiffened at the mention of her former suitor's name. She swallowed embarrassed by the foolish woman she had become, by her Minerva costume and her yearning for a man who did not even appear to like her.

"Any man who views dancing with a woman as an opportunity to be free with his hands is unworthy of the name gentleman," he said in a tone as harsh as a whip-crack.

Holly's eyes widened. "Are you being protective of me?"

His eyes smoldered behind the black silk mask. "Yes. I always take care of what's mine. King, country, castle…or wife."

Holly stumbled. "Your Bo Peep looked quite put out with you," she commented after she regained her footing, in an attempt to deflect attention.

"I was not a good partner. I found myself distracted by your plight."

"My plight? I assure you I had the situation well under control. As you observed, he was no gentleman, but I am quite capable of taking care of myself," she said indignantly.

Was that a smirk curling up the corners of his mouth?

Before she could decide, Rey twirled her a fraction too hard. Was everyone staring at her, or was it just the crawling insecurity that had dogged her ever since her catastrophic error of judgment with Lord Pickford that made it seem so? Either way, his manhandling, though technically more respectable in scope, was every bit as unwelcome as Lothario's had been. It was all she could manage not to yank her arms away from his grip and leave him there on the dance floor. It would serve him right. But then she wouldn't have the feel of his large, hard body swaying against hers. How confusing, to want his touch but not in the way she currently had it. His jaw had tightened. She wanted him to soften for her. She might as well embrace a boulder and ask for a kiss.

There were so many questions she wished to ask. Yet in this moment, words failed her, so she said nothing.

Instead, Holly let herself memorize the way her future husband's gloved palm burned against the indent of her waist. Her feet moved easily in his guidance. Turn, place her palm in his. Turn the other way, bow to the neighboring couple. Reverse direction. Repeat. Never in her life had Holly felt so rattled in the company of a man. How was she to charm him when he was made of granite?

Her heart sank. They were doomed, truly, if they couldn't even carry on a conversation. Where was the man who had called off their nuptials? That version of Rey Sharp had been equal parts compassion and strength. He was a man she could admire, even...

Love.

Having been denied her mother's approval for her entire life, Holly thirsted for approval like a sampling in a drought. Whatever his faults—and Lord Pickford was without a doubt vain, selfish, and obtuse—the beau she had chosen for herself had loved her for herself. Not in a romantic or physical sense, but without trying to change her. She wished he would write to her. Let her know he was all right, that he still cared. Not because Holly harbored any illusions of their coming together in marriage but because they had been genuine friends. He had made her feel adored, even if he hadn't actually loved her.

"Poor Bo Peep," Holly replied. "You ought to go and save her, the way you did for me. Not that I needed it, mind you."

Rey's expression hardened again as the smirk disappeared. "Of course not. If I was presumptuous in stepping in, please understand that I am sensitive to abuses of station. My mother was a maid in a fine house. My father was..." he bit off the end of his sentence. "I don't take kindly to men who take advantage of their position."

The song ended on that peculiar admission.

She had been absorbed in her own problems without considering why her husband had reacted with such force. "I was glad for your intervention," she called, but it was too late. Holly had hesitated a moment too long. The song had ended, and Rey left her alone. But she was not a woman to stand there, bereft. Holly's mouth flattened into a determined line. "You can't leave me hanging like that, Reynard Sharp," she muttered and stalked after him. "I don't take orders like one of your soldiers."

And blast the man, she never would.

"What did you mean back there?" Holly demanded of Reynard's broad back. Her heart had relocated to the base of her throat where it pounded annoyingly. He stiffened. She had ample time to admire the breadth of his shoulders and the way his short dark hair curled slightly into waves over the bands holding his mask. Rey's ears stuck out slightly at the tips. They were tinged a bright pink.

"What do you mean, what did I mean?" Finally, he turned around. Brown eyes as cool as fresh-turned earth in a summer garden met hers.

"About your mother." The hammering of her heart in her throat calmed. Holly was a long way from feeling like her normal self so she welcomed the seed of confidence sprouting up now.

Rey's eyes narrowed at the inner corner. What a strangely effective trick. It conveyed utter disdain with subtle and devastating precision. Holly swallowed. Undeterred, she said, "You said she was a maid."

He gave no reply though his squint narrowed further. She tried again. "If you think it matters to me, it doesn't. My mother is the only one who cares about breeding and parentage."

This was not strictly true. Her parents had been perfectly willing to marry her off to Finlay Weston last year. Holly had been convinced she could aim higher. Lord Pickford had already become her close confidant and friend. She had been certain it was only a matter of time before love blossomed between them. Holly had been wrong, but she had no regrets about not marrying Finn. How could she when her favorite cousin and best friend was so deliriously in love with him?

"Then why did you angle so hard to marry an earl?" Rey asked with deceptive softness.

Holly swallowed. "Because I thought it would get my mother to stop trying to control—"

"There you are!" A woman in a towering blonde coiffure topped with gold crown spikes swooped in, startling them both.

"Mother," Holly yelped. The Sun's gold-dusted brow furrowed.

"You aren't supposed to acknowledge me, Minerva. This is a masquerade," hissed her mother in a low tone. Turning to Rey, she beamed. "Now, dear mystery man, I have come to …. Do what?"

"Do something,"

"I am at your service, your ladyship." Rey bowed stiffly.

"Oh, I am no lady," Mrs. Mayweather tittered.

"Pardon my error," Rey responded with smooth reserve. It was as if a gear had notched into place. His expression softened. The hard lines bracketing his mouth faded. His eyes widened as fractionally as they had closed down a moment before. "I was blinded by your beauty. The sun is above such frivolous considerations as rank."

This made Mrs. Mayweather's mouth pucker with displeasure, for what good Englishman cared naught about rank? The order of society was, while permeable by the lucky few, everything that gave the country structure, backbone and moral fiber. Everyone sought to advance their position. "Aren't you a military man, sir?"

Rey's mouth crooked at the corners in a grimace of tolerance. "An excellent guess."

Holly sighed. What a stupid fiction, this pretense of not knowing one another. Her mother knew full well that Rey had been a soldier—although she knew very little about what he did with himself now. Her parents had been liberal in their displeasure with her downfall but in the process of constant shaming had neglected to share many facts about her beau. "Madam Aurora, if you don't mind, you are interrupting."

Her mother spoke tightly, as frosty as an arctic winter. "I won't let you botch this engagement, Minerva."

So much for the pretense of not knowing one another's identities.

"I've no idea what you mean," Rey interjected. "Minerva and I were just discussing…"

"Bo Peep's sheep," Holly blurted. She spied Amity making an awkward transfer of the bewildered animal back to its owner.

Her mother blinked. "How ingenious to bring an actual, real live lamb to a ball."

"Are you quite serious? Don't you mean, how asinine?" interjected Rey. Holly cast him an agonized smile. Her mother, taken aback at Rey's blunt words, sputtered.

"That is exactly what I said!" Mrs. Mayweather tapped him on the bicep with her fan. "It is *so* loud in here."

Holly bit her lower lip in embarrassment. She loved her mother. She hated the way her mother pretended so hard to be things she wasn't. The way Holly had pretended to be someone she wasn't to attract the attentions of Lord Pickford. Holly sighed. She was never going to forgive herself for unwittingly following in her mother's.

"Madam Aurora," Holly said loudly. "I believe your moon is seeking you." She gestured with her fan at her father, who sported a white domino decorated with a few strategically placed paste gems and a white suit with a midnight blue jacket and silver spangled waistcoat. She ought to better appreciate the genius of a sun and moon costume, but Holly was too attuned to the presence of her fiancé.

The prospect of Rey Sharp dressing up like a moon to her sun was unfathomable.

He regarded her warily as Mrs. Mayweather swanned over to her husband, leaving behind a trail of perfume. "I don't wish to discuss my family in the middle of a ball."

Holly dropped her gaze, chagrined. "When can we speak privately?"

"We will be partners for the scavenger hunt," Rey replied with a note of resignation that made her wince.

"If we are to marry five days hence, I need more than a few hours of conversation. I want…" Holly hesitated. "I want to know we won't hate one another a year from now. I won't marry you without a hint of real affection between us."

She dared not ask for love. That was far too much to hope for. Besides, a few days wasn't enough time for anyone to fall in love. But to come to an understanding? To gain a sense of a person's expectations for marriage? Surely, a few days was sufficient.

The perfect horizontal line of Rey's shoulders softened. He inhaled sharply. Then he leaned close and cupped her chin in his hand. His eyes blazed with dark fire from behind the black frame of his domino. His kiss was as hard as granite. Holly gasped against his mouth. Rey shifted, seeking entry with the touch of his tongue between her lips. She opened like a parched woman finding water in a desert. His kiss flooded through her entire body with rain sluicing through dry river bed. She moaned, wanting more.

Abruptly, he pulled away. Rey's chest rose and fell. His gaze of banked desire glanced off hers.

"Come to my room tonight," he spat, "I'll show you affection."

Holly gaped as Rey stalked away.

"Who are you?" she whispered after him. Her abdomen had gone soft but she felt his challenge like a blow.

"Are you all right?"

Holly startled. Amity and Finn looked worriedly at her. Weston's mouth, visible beneath his mask, was creased in a tight line.

"I'm fine. Truly." She shook her shoulders and pulled herself up. Holly's face warmed. "We had a moment of…"

"Passion?" Amity suggested. "He kissed you in the midst of a ball." She glanced around.

"I can't believe he'd do something like that. I thought I knew the man. Apologies, Holly, do you want me to have a word with him?" asked Finn with a scowl.

"No, it isn't necessary. We just need to spend some time together. I like him very much." It was another half-truth brightly told to uphold a fiction Holly wanted desperately to believe in. That they could come together, if not in love, then in peace. If she could figure out how to tap into the man's passions they might stand a chance at happiness.

※

Rey fell into his bedroom with bated breath. Fire crackled in the grate. Other than that, the room was lifeless.

Holly hadn't come. Had he genuinely expected her to? Not enough to prevent him from taking up one of the new arrival's invitation to the Arms pub in town, just two miles away by clear winter roads. It had been a relief to be amongst his plain-spoken peers again, although he had felt a difference even there. Their pockets jingled merrily with coins, and his companions had been attended eagerly by the barmaid. The well-endowed lass had cheerfully tolerated the five of them tossing mildly ribald jokes in her direction. She'd slapped one person's hand when he tried to sneak a squeeze of her breast, grinned, and brought a round on the house. Everyone had left satisfied.

Except Rey. He'd been silent all the way home, wondering whether Holly had tried to take him up on his lunatic offer to satisfy her curiosity. He hadn't believed a gently-reared woman would have the courage. But if any woman were to, it would be Holly.

He staggered a step or two toward his bed. The clock down the hallway chimed two in the morning. Masked partiers still filtered into the sleeping quarters in pairs or singly. The Stapletons were too respectable to permit any real scandals to play out under their roof. Rey fell onto the bed and kicked off his boot. It thunked against the door.

Respectable. That's what he was now. It was a good thing Holly wasn't here. He'd have ravished her given half an opportunity. That's how *respectable* he was.

No. He would have been sorely tempted, but he would have restrained himself. He was a knight now, or nearly so. Knights didn't ravish women, not even when they presented themselves in one's bedroom expressly for such a purpose.

Then again, he might never be granted a knighthood. Prinny was, after all, prone to forgetting. It would be entirely like the prince to dally and delay until the urgency of granting a boon had passed.

It is to your advantage to secure a wife of good breeding and better fortune, Wellington had advised him upon his departure from military service. Thanks to Holly's devotion to a man unfit to lick her boots, Rey had a chance to do just that. The problem was that he, too, was unfit to taste her footwear, much less her mouth. Rey fell back on the counterpane, rubbed his eyes with his fists, and groaned. Holly's taste lingered on his skin despite tankards of ale that should have replaced it hours ago. He hadn't managed to stop thinking about her for a single second.

Rey was falling in love with his future wife. Lord pity him, for as far as Rey could tell, Holly was still enamored of the man who had spurned her. Pickford, who was everything he was not. Rich. Titled. Accustomed to the minute politics of ballrooms that so easily tripped up unwary interlopers like himself. Maybe Holly would have been happier with a man who ignored her in bed but played to her strengths publicly, than with a man who wanted to worship her at night but didn't know how to make her happy outside of the bedroom.

On that unhappy thought, Rey gave in to sleep.

Chapter Seven

The morning after the excitement of the masked ball, only the natural larks were out of bed early—and Holly was a born night owl. She awoke to bright sunshine filtering through her window onto a tray of sweet breads, cold kippered salmon, butter, preserves, and boiled eggs. Ravenous, she rang for tea and set about getting ready for the day with the help of her maid. By the time she made her way down to the parlor, Lord and Lady Stapleton were handing out the rules of the scavenger hunt.

Holly spotted Reynard and edged her way over to stand next to him.

"Nice of you to make an appearance," he muttered. "I was afraid I'd have to do the list alone."

Holly blushed. "I'm here now. Good morning to you, dear…" She trailed off. With two kisses between them, there shouldn't be any awkwardness, yet she felt shyer than ever before. Worse, Reynard flinched at the appellation *dear*. It shouldn't feel like rejection. She *had* been too forward. Had she imagined the affection between them yesterday? Or the kiss in the library? Judging from the way his brow furrowed, indeed she had. Each time she thought they had taken a step forward together, he retreated back into his shell of disdain.

"We are looking for a pearl in a sprig of mistletoe." He examined the hand-lettered list in flowing scrawl.

Holly's gaze rose to the boughs of mistletoe adorning every doorway and mantle in the house. "We might be at that all morning." Indeed, other players were already standing on chairs to search through the tiny white berries in search of a paste pearl. "What's next on the list?"

"We're supposed to do it in order, aren't we?" Reynard protested, though he let her pluck the paper from his grasp.

"Nonsense. It's a scavenger hunt. We cross off each item as soon as we find it." Holly squinted at the letters. "Let's see, we need a bronze key, a silver thimble, a person with red hair, a person who has been to Scotland, a—"

"Found her! Everyone, here's the Holly!" Amity clapped and twirled, her eyes bright and dancing with mischief. Near her was Finlay, who laughed.

"True," Holly chuckled. Each year at Christmas, she could expect at least one joke about her name. "Cross that one off."

"You mean you can just dart around finding things willy nilly?" Reynard asked as if astounded.

"Of course. Haven't you ever played before?" Holly bit her tongue. "I'm sorry. I suppose if you haven't done a hunt before the rules aren't immediately obvious."

"Not even as a child?" Amity asked Reynard in surprise.

"Leave the man be, ladies," Finn interjected. "Army life is all about discipline. Is it any wonder our friend is perplexed by a freewheeling game?" He brushed a kiss against his wife's temple.

"As if you'd know anything about military life," Amity teased.

Holly tasted jealousy. Why couldn't it be easy for her and Rey, the way it was for Amity and Finlay?

"I can do this," Reynard declared, snatching back the list and making a firm pencil strike through the words "Holly bough."

"I think Holly needs to bow, to make it official," Amity said. Holly gave a flourish of her wrist and bent at the waist. When she came up, her fiancé's gaze bored daggers in her. For the love of Pete, couldn't she say or do anything right?

"Done!" Finally exclaimed. He gleefully crossed off the word, too. "It's too bad you didn't come down sooner, Holly. Lady Stapleton might have assigned us to be partners."

"We could work as a group of four," Amity offered. Wood scraped in the background. Their competitors had abandoned their examination of the foliage and darted off to other parts of the large house.

"No, thank you," Holly said briskly. If she was going to get to know her mercurial husband-to-be, they needed time together. Time to talk, and with luck, for more kissing. The thought that he hadn't once had the opportunity to be in a scavenger hunt as a child made part of her heart twist up. What a bleak existence it must have been. "We'll beat you fair and square, Mr. and Mrs. Weston, or my name isn't Holly Mayweather."

She thrust her chin high and stalked away in pretend ire. Finlay and Amity laughed, clasped hands, and headed toward the kitchens in search of a ginger errand boy. Holly knew this because she turned back at the doorway to glance over her shoulder and witnessed it.

Reynard remained rooted in place. She sighed. "Well, come on, then."

"Why didn't you take them up on their offer to work together?" Reynard asked.

"Because the only person I want to work with is you, Rey." Holly turned on her heel and stalked away before she could glimpse his reaction. Her heart beat quickly as if she had danced a reel, when all she had done was speak the truth of her desire. His heavier footfall soon caught up with her. "My maid probably has a silver thimble. A bronze key is tricky though. I have no idea what keys are made of, do you?"

"Holly."

The sound of her name on his lips made her stop short. "Yes?"

"I shouldn't have told you that about my mother, last night."

"Why not?" She demanded. "Did you think I'd never find out?"

Frustration pulled his brows into a frown. "No, it isn't that."

"My parents did intimate that your family was not typical gentry," she continued, softly, after glancing about to make sure there was no one to overhear them. "It does not matter to me."

"Holly. I let you think my upbringing was less than ideal. It was, in the sense that my mother was away working most of the time and my father had no interest in me, but my grandparents were caring and devoted people. I lacked for nothing. I have played scavenger hunts before, though not since I was a lad. I didn't recall that you could look for things out of order. That's all."

"Oh," she squeaked. Rey had come closer to as he spoke. They were in the parlor, alone. He did not touch her. It would have been better if he did, but instead, he loomed over her. Holly's eyes drifted closed as she imagined his hands at her waist—this time, without clothing. Warmth tightened her abdomen.

"You didn't come to my room last night."

"I tried to, after my sister was asleep," she whispered, "But you'd joined up with the lads and gone to the tavern in town."

"Really?" He closed his eyes. "I was a fool. I wish I had waited for you."

Holly released a breath she'd held unconsciously and smirked at him. "As do I. This is a house party. Doubtless we'll find another opportunity. They tend to be notorious for relaxed rules, even upstanding families like the Stapletons." Her cheeks were hot. "Now, let's go and find a blue garter."

"Yes. Right. Of course." Reynard was already on his way. She had to trot to catch up. "But, where?"

"Are you running away from me?" she demanded, huffing to keep up with him.

"Most assuredly not. Although I will note that retreat is a perfectly honorable way to survive a battle and win the war."

"We are not at war, Rey. Stop pretending as if we are." This made him pause mid-step.

"Right. We are partners in this mad escapade." He stared grumpily at the list of items to locate. "You don't happen to be wearing blue garters, do you?" Holly hiked up a fistful of her skirt and kicked out one leg, grinning. Rey clapped his palm over his face. "This isn't helping."

"As you see, plain garters," she confirmed. "Nothing pretty about them. However, I do know of a certain risqué portrait of a previous Lady Stapleton in which blue garters are prominently featured."

"I cannot believe you did that in the middle of the Stapleton's house," Rey groaned.

Holly clucked her tongue. "What did I say about relaxed rules? Now, come on, where's your competitive streak. Let's win this!"

❆

Rey's beer-fuzzed head didn't make keeping up with Holly's lightning-quick changes of mind any easier. She led him past the music room, where two other couples were searching the instruments. Giggling, she clasped his hand and led him around another corner. "I cannot imagine what they thought they'd find inside a French horn," she snorted.

Neither could he. "Is sleeping late every morning how you deal with staying out late every night?" he asked.

"One must sleep sometime," she smirked, prompting Rey's thoughts to take a turn for the salacious. The only thing he wanted to stay up late doing was parting Holly's sweet, pale thighs. Her mischievous flashing of garters had prompted impure, manly needs. Distracted, he hardly noticed the parade of dismal portraits lining the Stapleton's hallway until Holly pulled him into an alcove. "Here we go. Do you see them?"

"What is this?" he demanded, aghast at the sheer ridiculousness of the portrait. In the center was a distinctly nude woman artfully draped in a gauzy white gown with a blue belt and a matching ribbon tied around her upper thigh.

"This delightful confection is the previous Lord and Lady Stapleton dressed as Oberon and Titania from *A Midsummer Night's Dream*."

He bent to peer at the plaque affixed to the frame. "'The Wedding of Oberon to Titania,'" Rey read. "What on earth is this monstrosity?"

"A couple of generations ago, Lord Stapleton fell in love with an actress. Titania was her famed role. He had this commissioned after his First Lady Stapleton passed and he married his actress." Holly couldn't keep the mirth out of her voice. "It's atrocious, isn't it?"

"The worst painting I have ever seen."

"My godparents have probably forgotten all about it,"

Holly laughed. "I can't wait to see their faces when we tell them where we found the blue garter—do write it down, and be specific."

Rey produced the pencil and scavenger hunt list from his pocket and complied. "Have you read the play?" he asked idly, scribbling.

"It's one of my favorites. Especially the line, 'Though she be but little, she is fierce!' I used to run about screaming that at my brothers when they annoyed me. I had it memorized by the time I was ten."

"The entire thing?"

"Every line, by rote," she confirmed, bouncing impatiently on her toes.

"I thought you didn't like books." His task finished, Rey pocketed the pencil and list and turned to face his mysterious, exasperating wife.

"Why not?" she asked, puzzled.

"When we were in the library, you didn't seem impressed by all the books. It's the finest collection I've ever seen." Even to his own ears, Rey's response sounded presumptive.

"I had seen it before," Holly said reproachfully. Her energetic bouncing stopped. "Besides, I was more interested in that moment in you than in rereading a book, no matter how beloved."

"You...love history?" Rey couldn't quite grasp the notion that Holly had interests of her own. To his deepening consternation, she nodded.

"Oh, yes. Shakespeare is my favorite author of all. I'm especially partial to his sonnets. I've never heard words as poetic as his in all the English language. *Let me not to the marriage of true minds/Admit impediments. Love is not love/Which alters when in alteration finds/Or bends with the remover to remove.* Nor French, come to think of it. I am generally partial to French poetry. Do you enjoy reading?"

She liked books. She read French. How had he neglected to learn these rudimentary facts about her? Rey shook his head.

"No? Pity. Well, we shall find other entertainments to enjoy together. Music, perhaps. Come on, we still have half the list to find. Let's get searching!"

Before he could find the words to explain himself, Rey found himself dragged by his small, mighty, and ever-surprising fiancée. They did not win the scavenger hunt. Stymied by the bronze key, he and Holly rejoined their friends and were unsurprised to discover the prize had gone to another couple. Holly's disappointment at losing was tempered when she announced where they had located the blue garter. The entire room burst into laughter. Even Rey grinned at the Stapleton's mild embarrassment when they were reminded of their ancestor's poor taste.

"I do enjoy reading, you know," he blurted when the rest of the party had dissipated. "Why do you think I asked if you had seen the library?" She hadn't been quite honest with him, Rey realized.

"Because it's private and convenient for kissing?" she smirked impishly. "Which is something I hope you'll do more of after we are married two days hence."

Heat seared the tips of his ears. He hadn't imagined it. Holly had liked kissing him. It was almost enough to make him forget how easily she stretched the truth whenever it suited her—but not quite.

Chapter Eight

Reynard's second wedding day dawned cloudy. He tried not to take it as a sign.

His valet helped him into a muted buff waistcoat with gold embroidery and a Paris green jacket. Reynard hated it on sight. "No. The navy."

"Sir, if you please, emerald honors the holiday season—"

"The *navy*," he insisted.

His affronted servant sulked. "At least permit me to recommend the bottle green as a nod to the holiday."

"You have done your duty in advising me on my sartorial selections. The navy suffices." It was comfortable, if not celebratory. Familiar. Holly would hate it.

"Never mind. The bottle green, then." His valet's relief was palpable. Why did any man need so many clothes? Sumptuous silk or linen cravats. Irish linen underthings. Superfine wool and ridiculous things called opera pumps. What was wrong with a pair of good Cordoba leather boots, anyway? They had served him well in his years fighting Napoleon.

The bottle green, several shades darker and bluer than the

poisonous-looking emerald, represented a decent compromise between the severity of the navy and the exuberance of the brighter Paris green. It became a last-minute representation of his hopes for their union. Mutual compromise. A gesture of goodwill. But would Holly understand his message?

Reynard blew out a gusty sigh. Of course she wouldn't. She wasn't in the room, and it was an article of clothing, not a love note. For a war hero noted for his strategic thinking, he turned awfully muddle-brained around Holly Mayweather. "If we must make a nod to the season, why not my regimental uniform?"

His valet's thin lips disappeared into a flat line of disapproval. "If you wish it, sir."

"Is red with gold trim not festive?" Rey asked.

"Very much so." There was no pleasing the man, so he decided to stop trying. He was quickly garbed in his military finery. It was like stepping into an old skin. For the first time since his arrival, Reynard's confidence returned. His spine straightened and his shoulders fell away from his ears. In the vestibule to the Stapleton's private chapel he found Finlay and Amity Weston, the Stapletons, and the Mayweathers. Mr. and Mrs. Mayweather looked on as a string trio played a brief tune. He swallowed and took his place before the vicar. The last time they had stood before this unsmiling and serious vicar, Reynard had been moments away from halting the ceremony. That had required considerable fortitude of spirit.

Why didn't this morning feel any different?

It ought to, but curiously he felt more nervous now. Waiting for the words that would bind him to the teasing minx for life, a strange feeling of hope swelled and gathered in his breast. Within minutes, the vicar would pronounce the blessing that gave him access to Holly's delectable body.

Reynard swallowed. More than any social polish or connections or dowry she brought to their union, he wanted *her*.

Her humor. Her lightheartedness. All of it.

The musicians changed songs, and soon Holly's veiled form drifted into view. He tucked her gloved hand into his elbow. The vicar droned on, words that ought to be seared into his brain but which passed over him without meaning. Because Reynard knew that despite the past week of stolen kisses and twenty questions and teasing scavenger hunts, he had not wooed his would-be wife the way she wanted. Certainly, he had not earned her hand in marriage.

"Do you take this Miss Holly Mayweather to be your lawfully wedded wife?"

"Yes," Reynard replied, surprised at his own calmness.

"Do you, Miss Holly Mayweather, take this man—"

"Not yet."

There was a groan from somewhere behind them. The vicar blinked. "I beg your pardon?"

Holly extracted her hand from his elbow and fought to turn back the veil. "Mr. Sharp and I are not finished courting," she burst out the moment her face was free of the lace and netting. A high blush spread over her cheeks.

The vicar regarded them as a shepherd might a pair of wayward lambs straying from his flock—as in, he was ten seconds from hooking them around the neck. "A week was not enough for Mr. Sharp to win your affections, Miss Mayweather?"

His dire tone called into question Reynard's manhood and simultaneously implied that Holly was too high at the instep. Holly's blush deepened. "It's not that, sir. We need a few more days to…" She trailed off and cast him a pleading glance.

Much as he loathed to do so, Reynard knew what he had to do.

"We understand the importance of this commitment and are approaching it with the utmost seriousness," he said.

"Is there a specific reason to delay?" asked the vicar suspiciously.

"Yes," Holly said, at the same time that Reynard said "No."

They glanced at one another. He found reproach in his bride's gaze. "Rey, I cannot marry someone who is so determined to believe the worst about me. I haven't won your trust, and to be honest, you haven't won mine."

Her blue eyes bored into him. It was true. He'd known it deep down that this was not the morning yet he had moved forward anyway. "What have I done wrong, Holly?"

"I refuse to marry in suspicion and doubt. I have tried, as best I can, to tame my tongue and yet I still feel as though your first instinct is to believe the worst in me. For example, thinking I didn't like books."

"I—" Rey swallowed hard. "It's not you, Holly. I'm trained not to trust anyone easily. I can't simply set it aside because you tell me to."

"But if you can't trust me, why would you want to marry me?"

Because I thought I could endure a loveless marriage, even an unfaithful one. But that was before I met you. Fortunately, his jaw was too tense to permit him to speak the words out loud. "You're right." He swallowed hard. "For the past week, we have come to know one another, but not yet to understand and trust. I agree with Holly's assessment. We need more time."

Most of all, he needed to find a way to keep her by his side forever. Everything he had believed about the sort of marriage they might have had gone out the window within the span of a few days. Rey needed a new strategy to reassert his control over his wayward wife. Especially now that he knew how much she could hurt him with a betrayal.

"Very well," sighed the vicar ponderously. "I shall grant you one final reprieve. You must exercise the special license before its expiration on January 5th. Otherwise, you must apply for a new marriage license. Do you understand?"

"Yes, sir," Reynard and Holly replied in unison. At last, they were in agreement on something.

The Mayweathers clucked and scolded their daughter all the way back up the short aisle way. Stunned by the brief and interrupted ceremony, Reynard remained rooted in place and lost in thought.

How had he let her believe he doubted her?

Because he *had* doubted her, at least at first. And he'd never done much to correct her perceptions even though his opinion of her *had* changed a great deal during the past week.

"Tough break, lad," Finlay said, clapping him on the arm. Amity had gone with her aunt and cousin, presumably to try and smooth things over. "I guess she wanted to exact revenge upon you for leaving her at the altar a week ago. Turnabout being fair play and all."

"She's not like that," Reynard protested, but his friend scoffed. They sauntered away from the chapel and back toward the main castle.

"Of course she is," Finlay said. "Fortunately for us, her antics are easy to spot from a mile distance. A keen planner like you ought to be able to outwit her next time." He chuckled.

"You don't know her," Rey declared with vehemence that shocked them both. "Not as well as you think."

"Oh, and you've figured her out after a few days' company?"

Rey halted mid-stride. "You know what, Finn? I am glad

you didn't marry Holly. The two of you together would have been a catastrophe."

"That makes two of us," his friend declared. "I couldn't have borne her constant need for attention. Fickle, shallow, and faithless, who needs it?"

"If Holly is so faithless, why did she wait two years for a man who never intended to marry her?" Rey demanded. "And furthermore, why would you suggest I marry such a woman? It was you and Amity who helped arrange our match, after all."

"Pickford? Well, if she were willing to tolerate his male lovers in exchange for a title, I hardly see how that proves your point—" sputtered Finn before Rey cut him off mid-sentence.

"She didn't know. Everyone assumed Holly was after Pickford's title, but did anyone bother to whisper a hint of warning? No. For three entire months while you were together enjoying the Season, her own cousin's husband couldn't be trusted to warn her of the danger to her reputation."

Finlay hung his head.

"Holly reads poetry and histories. She likes to dance and speaks French and plays piano admirably. She is bright and charming and if she finds London more stimulating than the slower pace of country living, that is a mark of lively intelligence and keen curiosity, not a reason for censure." Reynard had recovered his equilibrium, and with it, his temper calmed. Why hadn't he remembered earlier that a strategy was only as good as one's insights into the opposing side's motivations?

"Well, Sharp, it appears you have Holly all figured out." Finlay stepped back, half-turned, and made as if to speak. "I want you to know I have nothing but affection for my wife's cousin. I wish you both much happiness. Should your union ever come to pass, of course."

His friend turned and strode quickly away before Reynard could respond. Leaving him to ponder the obvious question alone.

What if he was wrong about Holly?

❉

"I am not flighty." Holly felt her lower lip protrude ever so slightly and willed it back from a habitual pout.

"I didn't say you were." Amity had perched herself in a window seat in the morning room which overlooked the snow-covered landscape, knees bent beneath her. Outside, children tossed snowballs and fashioned lumpy snowmen out of rolled snow and sticks.

"But you implied it," Holly said with a hint of accusation. Her cousin glanced away. One strand of dark hair brushed over Amity's forehead. When she looked up again there was guilt in her eyes. "Amity, I have never felt more confident of anything in my life. I want Reynard Sharp to be my husband."

"Do you love him?" Amity asked thoughtfully.

This time, it was Holly who turned away. She had paced the same path her feet had trod for the past quarter-hour. "Yes," she said after another pass by the wingback chair upholstered in *Bois de Citron* chintz. "I love him."

I think—at least, I hope that's what this feeling is. The jangly anticipation as though her nerves were strung with bells, all chiming dissonantly whenever Rey walked into a room. The way his brooding scowl softened when she teased him out of seriousness into a reluctant laugh lit her from the inside. She hadn't known there was so much dark, empty loneliness in her heart before the past week. When Rey had begun to fill it by challenging her in ways no one else had ever cared to do. Plus, just thinking about his kisses made her cheeks hot. Lord Pickford had never made her feel this way.

"Then why, why, *why* did you refuse him this morning?" Amity almost shouted. She fisted her crisp white muslin skirt. "You could have been locked away in connubial bliss at this very moment."

Holly froze. Amity never raised her voice. Perhaps her plan to seduce her husband wasn't as clever as it had seemed last night when she had spent hours awake in bed, planning it. "Because if we had married this morning, he wouldn't respect me."

Amity groaned and dropped her face into one palm. "Holly Mayweather, I do not comprehend a thing you're saying."

"Let me explain."

"Please, by all means. We've at least an hour before tea."

"Shall I ring for some and we can take it here, in the sitting room?" Holly asked.

Amity went to the bell pull. "It sounds as though this might take a while."

They huddled together in the cramped window seat. "Hear me out, Amity."

"I'm listening."

"Reynard Sharp, being a military man, naturally prefers order and clear directions."

"Yes, and?" prompted Amity.

Holly nervously brushed a curl behind her ear before continuing. "If I don't show him that he cannot order me around like one of Wellington's soldiers before we marry, I will lose all leverage to make him see me as an equal partner after our vows are spoken."

Amity regarded her somberly. "Don't you trust him?"

"With my life. But surely you know by now that in a

marriage there are many compromises to make. I cannot be happy with any man who believes he can compel me to behave a certain way. I want to be his wife, and I want to make him happy, but I cannot give up every delight in life to accomplish that. I need him to show me he can meet me halfway."

"What happens if he can't, or won't?" asked Amity softly.

"Then...then I shall have to resign myself to spinsterhood," Holly replied. "At least I won't turn into my mother." The last part came out in a mumble. Amity clearly possessed keen ears, however.

"What do you mean about turning into your mother?"

Holly jumped off the seat. "Oh, look, tea." They spent a few minutes dishing tea and removed themselves from the window to the settee with a small table laden with a pot of tea, small sandwiches and tiny pies. "I want what you and Finlay have, Amity. Is that so much to ask?"

"What did you mean by that comment about your mother?" her cousin pressed, fixing her with a stern look.

Holly sighed. "My mother had so many interests before she married. I know she and Father adore one another, and she wouldn't change a thing about her life given the choice, but haven't you noticed how she schemes to arrange people's lives into marriage?"

"Well, yes, I rather had," Amity said wryly. She pursed her lips to blow on her hot tea. "Having been the subject of her ill-advised matchmaking."

"My mother was a bit of a bluestocking before she married my father. He ordered her to give up her love of books and become more...more..." Holly swallowed. "Social. No more discussions of philosophy, no debates. Just parties and dancing—which, as it happens, my mother also loves. But she has channeled all of that energy into replicating her happiness for others. I refuse to let that happen to me."

Amity regarded her soberly. "Holly. You could never be like your mother. You have generosity and tact, even when you choose not to apply them to a given situation."

Holly ignored the backhanded compliment. Amity had certainly become much more forthright since marrying Finn. "The point is, I cannot adapt myself to endless afternoons of needlepoint and wasting away in the countryside. If Rey cannot agree to spend some part of the year in town, then I cannot become his wife. It is better to know now than ten years from now, when there is no hope for change."

Holly was an optimist at heart but she was also pragmatic. Spending a few weeks in the country always left her chafing at the sameness of scenery and company. Though, come to think of it, she hadn't experienced that claustrophobic feeling since the arrival of more guests at the Stapleton's. It was hardly terrible being cooped up in the countryside as long as it didn't mean being alone with her mother and father trying to shoehorn the Mayweather siblings—or their friends—into inappropriate matches. It was the lack of escape she abhorred.

"I suppose I should tell you now that Finlay and I have agreed to spend the season in London again this spring. If your marriage to Mr. Sharp does not come to pass, you could join us. No one would blink to have my cousin stay with us, even if there's a whisper of scandal…" Amity's mouth closed in horror. "I don't believe there is the slightest possibility that this will result in a broken engagement, of course."

"But there is." Holly swallowed. "You know there is. I appreciate your offer but you and Finn deserve to explore on your own. I don't fancy being a third wheel again. Besides, it won't be necessary, because I intend to seduce my husband into wanting to make me happy."

"Oh?" Amity arched one brow, conspiratorially. "How do you intend to accomplish that?"

Chapter Nine

To be friendless at a house party was not a position Reynard much enjoyed.

Amity had been ensconced with her cousin all afternoon yesterday. Finlay had cast him a flinty glare before riding off alone for the morning's fox hunt. Reynard had followed the group for a mile or two, then turned around and let his horse meander back to the barn. He had tried the library, but Holly was nowhere to be found until supper, when she cast him impish glances across the crowded table. Maddening woman. How was he to seduce his wife when she was unavailable?

After the fox hunt a hearty late breakfast was served, Reynard nabbed a roll and escaped before the main party arrived back from the barn and stumbled upon a group of ladies lounging in the morning room.

"My son-in-law-to-be," Mrs. Mayweather exclaimed. "That is, if my daughter ever comes to her senses." Her blond hair was piled onto the crown of her head. Tendrils dangled elegantly around her ears. Her gown was a soft reddish brown that his valet would undoubtedly describe with some fantastical botanic moniker like *sorrel* or *coquelicot*. A contrasting shawl in Pomona green draped over her shoulders.

A comfortably proportioned woman occupying the nearby settee clucked her tongue sympathetically. "Wish for sons, Mrs. Weston. Wish for sons."

"Girls are nothing but trouble. Expensive to raise and marry off and willful to boot, the lot of them," a third woman added. Reynard regarded his would-be mother-in-law in horror.

"Were you not once girls?" he asked. The temperature in the room instantly dropped several degrees. Amity was curled into a chair with a book propped open on her lap. Apparently he had wandered into a married-ladies-only discussion.

"Yes, and I was the epitome of trouble," Mrs. Mayweather replied after a moment of stunned silence. When she laughed there was an edge to the practiced tinkling. "I loved books and poetry and long discussions of thoroughly disgraceful ideas about women's liberty. Can you even imagine?" She laughed again with a brittleness that belied her words. "What a fool I was."

"I loved dancing," the fat woman added with a wistful sigh. "But my husband doesn't enjoy it."

"You could have danced with other partners," Reynard pointed out.

"Yes, but he didn't like that either," she replied sadly, and reached for another biscuit. "Jealous, a bit. Not that I mind."

"I haven't changed for my husband," Amity spoke up, a bit shyly.

"That's what you think," Mrs. Mayweather countered. "We all change for our husbands, and it is for the better. I will be a happy woman the day my children are all safely wed." Brow furrowed, she added "Especially Holly."

Amity cast him a pleading look. Reynard understood instantly. "Speaking of whom. Do you have any idea where I might find my beloved bride?"

The women released a collective gasp as though the very idea of a man seeking out his wife-to-be's company was the most romantic thing they had ever heard.

"Why, yes, I shall take you to her." Amity was out of her chair and at his side in an instant. He offered her his arm, and she took it. The instant they were out of earshot, Mrs. Weston bent close to whisper "I could hardly stand their company for another instant. Thank you for providing me with an excuse to leave, Mr. Sharp."

"It comes at a price," he pointed out. "I need to know where Holly has been hiding out ever since our second attempted marriage yesterday."

Amity skipped a single step. Amusement animated her quietly pretty features. "Oh, she has been preparing."

"Preparing for what?"

"For you," Amity replied, unhelpfully. "Come along. I'll show you."

Amity led the way past room after room crowded with people playing charades or whist, taking in a brandy and cigar or otherwise occupying themselves. Reynard's guide pushed past a heavy wood door that looked to have been fashioned hundreds of years before. He had to duck to pass through it.

"Where are you taking me?" he asked.

"You'll see." Amity plucked a glass-enclosed lantern from a hook on the wall and began to mount a seemingly endless spiral stairway. Had he been an inch taller, Reynard would have banged his head against the ceiling. They tramped up the stairs in rhythm. Leather soles scraped against old stone. Grooves had formed where a thousand footsteps had come before them. The cold and clammy air clung to his skin. Despite this, he perspired lightly under his jacket—the bottle green, tonight, at the behest of his valet. Although it could not have been more than a few minutes, it felt as though an eternity had passed before his friend's wife paused at a small landing. She gestured to another old wood door on black hinges. Candlelight flickered from inside. "Go on. She's waiting for you."

Amity gave him a small, knowing smile, turned, and swept down the narrow staircase.

The hinges creaked as he nudged the door open. His entire body was on full alert. This felt too much like an assassination attempt. But who would attempt such a thing? The war was over. An attack would be pointless. Besides, this was…

Holly. Reynard's body tightened at the sight of her. Had he been stunned and tongue-tied by her beauty on first sight? Yes. This was far worse. His bride reclined on a divan piled high with plump pillows and topped with a red brocade coverlet. Fat candles under glass sat on the floor, warming the small space and bathing it in red-tinged light. She twirled one blond curl around her finger.

"Reynard," she purred. He choked. Facedown on the bed beside her lay a book. The gilt spine read *Shakespeare: Sonnets of Love and Devotion. A Collection*. If Reynard retained any lingering doubts about her interest in poetry, the book sealed it. "I've been waiting for you."

"So, I see," he managed to croak past dry lips. A thin night rail skimmed over her naked body. The flickering candlelight made it almost transparent. The outline of her small pink nipples tented the fabric. A small whimper may have escaped. Forget spies and guns and armies—one woman had brought him to his knees.

"It's been difficult to find time together without people watching. I made arrangements to borrow this tower for the evening," Holly explained. Her feet were encased in dainty white slippers with soft leather soles. Perfect for sneaking around the house in silence. "The same Lady Stapleton used it as a practice room. The Orientalist decor is her choosing. Gaudy, isn't it?" She shivered, whether in distaste for the decor or from the cold or in fear of the consequences if they were found out, he couldn't say. Assuming they married, no one would think much of it. Couples often anticipated their wedding vows. But if they were discovered and failed to marry before Twelfth Night, Holly would be well and truly ruined. No wonder her voice trembled.

"Miss Mayweather, your strategy for seduction would impress Wellington himself," Reynard complimented her. Her expression brightened. His anxiety eased instantly. Maybe Holly's instincts were right. All they needed was a bit of uninterrupted time to get to know one another better. Intimately, even. A physical release of the simmering tension between them would help matters immensely. His abdomen tightened with anticipation. He dropped onto a corner of the divan. Holly sat up, legs tucked beneath her, pretty feet disappearing beneath the hem of her white gown. "Holly. Permit me to be frank with you."

"I vastly prefer it to dissembling."

Reynard brushed her hair back from her face, then cupped her chin. "As do I. Tell me why you refused me, love."

She shuddered. Her delicate tremble raced up his palm. Love would be her nickname, then. Perhaps, in time, she might bestow one on him. Rey decided he'd like that—immensely.

After the tip of her tongue swept her lower lip, Holly said, "I cannot marry you if you expect obedience. Loyalty, affection, fidelity, all these I will lay at your feet. All I ask in return is—" she broke off. After a deep inhalation she continued, "Don't treat me like one of your soldiers. I am not yours to command, even as a wife."

Reynard had dropped his hand and now leaned back on his palms. "Have I done that, love?"

Her bravery softened. "Yes. I have felt as though you've been trying to change who I am. I thought you hated me on sight. But now I've realized we were locked in a dance of wills. Either you are commanding, or you're following me as if I am. I shall never forget that deep scowl. Or the way you could barely look at me. You were so severe. Never laughing, never light. Whereas I was born to speak all mirth and no matter."

"Shakespeare. Beatrice." Reynard recognized her reference.

"She is my favorite character in literature. I wanted to dress as Beatrice for the masquerade, but mother thought no one would recognize my costume." Holly drew her knees up inside her nightgown and rested her chin on top. "I like it when you call me 'love.'"

"I shall be certain to do so every day. Since we are speaking our hearts this evening..." He paused. "The first time I laid eyes on you, Holly, I thought my fortune was too good to be true. I was blinded and tongue-tied by your beauty."

"That's the silliest thing I have ever heard," Holly replied, blushing fiercely as if no man had ever given her a compliment before. Reynard felt the corner of his mouth pull up in a lopsided smirk.

"No, it's true, love." He adored the way her blue eyes darted at him every time he said it, half-suspicious, half-yearning. "I was convinced that no woman as pretty as you could be willing to marry a perfect stranger on no acquaintance whatsoever unless she was hiding something. I was determined to ferret out your dirtiest secrets."

Holly laughed. "I haven't any. Well, none you haven't already heard."

"I believe you now," Reynard said, rolling back onto the pile of cushions. "But at the time, I was skeptical. One does not spend over a decade in service to the Crown devising ways to outwit Napoleon's armies on the basis of limited information, without developing a certain degree of mistrust."

"But you had barely met me. How could you distrust me?" Holly asked.

For a woman with a reputation as a city sophisticate, she was such an innocent. "It was instinct. Wrong-headed, but due in no part to your actions. You see, love, I was born to a maid in an earl's house and the man's son. On the wrong side of the blanket so they say. A bastard."

"I know, you've told me this before."

"Patience, dear heart." How to speak his heart when he had spent so long silencing it? "People like your family and your friends have often held me in contempt for the circumstances of my birth. I have been advised to expect notice of receiving the knighthood and an accompanying property. It is in poor condition. It will require a great deal of work to make it habitable. The land provides an income from rents but the amount is less than will be needed to improve the main house. I needed a wife with a dowry sizable enough to fill the gap. I had resigned myself to a companionable marriage to a woman I hoped would be tolerable enough. I did not believe the Westons' reports of your beauty. Imagine my surprise on the day we met. I have never been so tongue-tied in my life. You see, good things do not happen to me. There is always a fly in the soup, a worm in the apple, or a taint to the gift."

"Such as receiving a dilapidated house on a scrap of land as an ostensible reward for your service to the crown," Holly declared indignantly.

"Exactly. So, your damaged reputation—I accepted it as

part of the bargain. I further expected a plain-featured wife with a churlish temper."

"Well, I certainly have a sharp tongue," Holly chuckled a little sadly.

"Which you use to make people laugh. I never once imagined I could have a charming, witty, intelligent wife to keep me company in my dotage. I hadn't the slightest idea what to make of you at first. I was determined to believe every bad thing about you, real or imagined." He swallowed and cupped her cheek. "I decided on sight that I didn't deserve you. Then I set about proving myself right."

The pad of his thumb stroked over skin as soft as rose petals. A shiver crawled up his spine. Holly's gentle sigh whispered against his palm. When he met her gaze, he found empathy. Caring. A sweetness that threatened to crack his heart in two. It made him ache with need to be truly worthy of her. Reynard wanted to belong in her world of levity and wisecracks, and frivolous entertainment enjoyed without guilt.

He was so tired of his guilt. Self-reproach that he had not been enough to bring his father and mother together. As unlikely as it was that an earl's son would ever marry a chambermaid, it wasn't unheard of. As a child, he had believed that if he could prove to his father what a good boy he was, his parents might fall in love. It had left him painfully resentful each time his father disappointed him. He hadn't realized how much of that he had carried with him, lugging his anger and heartbreak over hundreds of miles and entire continents. But tonight, he was ready to let that go.

Nothing said he belonged like Holly's welcoming kiss. A rustle of silk was all the warning he had before the soft weight of woman clambered into his embrace. There was no elegance to Holly's movements now. Her artlessness brought a grin to his lips just before her mouth landed on his.

Reynard buried his hands in her thick blond curls. He tilted her face just the right way to tease the bow of her upper lip with his tongue. Holly sighed and tried to wriggle closer. He kissed her firmly, with all the gentleness he possessed. She stilled in his arms, one hand braced against his chest and using the other to prop herself up. They half-reclined, kissing with closed-mouth intimacy, until she settled against his chest. He flipped her onto her back. Holly yelped in surprise.

"See? I can be playful," he teased, propping himself on one arm.

"Mr. Sharp, I am all surprise," she winked, grinning.

"I am full of surprises. Wellington's Fox, they called me. The French." Reynard winced inwardly. He had despised that nickname.

"Is that so?" she giggled, and suddenly, it was all right. He could trust her with his secrets. Let down his guard. Be himself. Holly did not want to judge him, she wanted to explore him, apparently—which he did not mind in the least. Her busy hands stroked the contours of his upper arm. He liked the way she traced his body with curious touches. He liked kissing her more, however. "Indeed. I've another surprise for you."

"Oh?" She sat halfway up, blue eyes sparkling with interest. Rey smoothed her hair back from her face, then brought his mouth to hers again. This time they met with open-hunger. Tongue met tongue in a dance as old as time. Sensuous and learning. He skimmed his hand down her ribs. When she arched against his palm, Reynard captured her beaded nipple between his thumb and forefinger. She gasped and clutched the back of his head. "Rey…I…"

"Keep going?" he asked, teasing the bud through the thin linen of her night dress.

"Yes. More," she sighed.

Reynard took his time. He nipped his way down her

throat, tasting, licking, inhaling her sweetly feminine musk. He shifted so as to not frighten or embarrass her with the hard ridge of his fully aroused cock. They would do nothing more than what she wanted tonight. If she wished to save the wedding night for tomorrow, after their union was formalized, so be it. He wasn't an animal. He could control himself.

He dipped his hand into her bodice. One pert breast popped free, pink-tipped and begging for his touch. Reynard caught her gaze as he swirled his tongue around the tiny nub. Her eyes widened with wonder. "Oh, yes," she breathed.

Assured of his welcome, he continued to worship her breast with his mouth while palming the other. Her moans were more satisfying than any pleasure he could imagine. His wife. Adoring him nearly as much as he adored her.

Abruptly, she writhed away, panting slightly as she sat up. Reynard bolted upright. Had he done something wrong? Misinterpreted?

"I want to be closer to you," she whispered. The silk robe slithered away from her shoulders. Her arms crossed, tugged, and the night rail was discarded in a quick movement. He sat there, stunned, at the vision of his naked wife.

Not wife, but almost.

"Say something," she whispered.

"You are the most beautiful woman I have ever seen." His throat was tight and raw.

Shy delight crinkled her eyes at the corners. "Let me see you, Rey."

Her hands were already at the placket of his shirt fumbling the shirt studs free. Reynard let her, unable to resist. He helped her free him from his waistcoat and the rest of his upper garments. His hard ridge was impossible to ignore now. The thought of burying himself inside Holly sent a sparks up his spine. Not yet. Not now.

But soon.

Chapter Ten

This man was hers.

Holly nibbled her lower lip in disbelief. Had she thought him severe? Yes, naive fool that she was. But she had been wrong. Reynard Sharp's smoldering, broody handsomeness was intensity, not judgment. Yet another way in which she had fooled herself by believing in her own sophistication.

How much wider would her world have been if she had stopped trying to live up to artificial standards and simply enjoyed London, without trying to pretend she was a better, wittier version of Holly Mayweather, to cover up her fear of inadequacy. Yes, her mother played a role in making her feel that way. But there had also been her own eagerness to prove herself as a debutante. To young girl, that had meant marrying into a title. How bewildering to think she might get what she had wanted, after all. She no longer cared about the honorific. Only the man.

"How did this happen?" she asked, tracing the white line of a knife cut along his ribcage.

"One of Bonaparte's spies thought he had the drop on

me." His mouth quirked up. "In truth, he nearly did. It was a close call."

"And this?" A puckered web of raised skin punctuated the area an inch below his collar bone. In between were ridges of muscle flecked with whorls of dark hair. The sight of two small, flat nipples made her insides turn soft.

"A bullet in the shoulder. It was a clean wound. Healed easily."

"It's a brutal business, war." she said regretfully. Before he could respond, she bent down to press a kiss to the old wound. Reynard gathered her hair and gently urged her face upward. Holly shivered at the newness of skin against skin.

"Let's not speak of it," Reynard whispered in her ear. "We've better uses for our tongues." He nipped her earlobe. Holly's bones melted. Her limbs were rubbery and weak as she clutched the crisp strands of his dark hair. His breath skimmed over her neck between open-mouth kisses. A long-denied desire clutched at her abdomen.

"You make me wanton," she whispered against the top of his head. He had worked his way down to savor the tips of her breasts again. The angle deprived her of the view she had so enjoyed moments before, although it presented her with a new view of his broad shoulders and back. She stroked her palm down the indentations of his spine. He shivered beneath her touch.

"I promise you the nightly opportunity to be as wanton as you wish, as soon as the ink is dry on our marriage license."

Holly pulled back. It required some effort, as Reynard had not paused in his efforts to drive her mad with passion. Going against her own instincts was never easy. Yet she managed. "I do not wish to wait."

As hard as she tried to sound commanding, she instead sounded mortifyingly petulant. She was not a child. She was a grown woman, as evidenced by her nakedness before her almost-husband—who groaned and sagged against the cushions. "You're going to be the death of me, love."

His posture left the interesting ridge of his arousal within reach. Holly gripped him and stroked over the layers of wool and linen. Rey half-sighed, half groaned. "You aren't going to let this go, are you."

"Metaphorically or literally?" Holly asked as she stroked the mysterious bulge with interest. She had seen naked penises on horses and little boys, or the occasional hound, of course. On statues they were typically concealed with minuscule fig leaves. Her husband's appendage was alarmingly closer to the equine example. That was supposed to go inside her?

How...uncomfortable. Yet she wanted it.

Reynard emitted a squeak that sounded suspiciously like a whimper. Fascinating. What had she said that so unnerved him? She squeezed his hard length experimentally. This time he jerked upright and manacled her wrists in his large hands. "Stop."

"Of course. I'm sorry. Was I hurting you?" Oh no, she'd done it wrong. How very like her to bumble forward with every good intention and find herself in a muddle. He let go. Holly tucked her hands under her knees.

"No," he gritted out. "I would very much like to discard these blasted trousers and give you everything you're asking for."

"Then...why don't you?" It made no sense. He had stated that he wanted to...to...make the beast with two backs, as Shakespeare had phrased it.

Another long-suffering whimper from her not-quite-husband. He buried his face in his hands. "Because, Holly, we aren't married."

"But we're going to be. Does a day or two make so much difference?" She shifted closer.

"It's the principle, love."

"We are to be married *in principle*, darling." Two could play at this game of leveraging affectionate nicknames. His head popped up. He clasped her behind the back of the neck and kissed her roughly.

"Say that again."

"Darling," she gasped. Her lips were full and roughened from his kisses.

"You are impossible." This time, though, he chuckled softly.

"That's why you love me," she countered. "Besides, if we are caught up here, or making our way back down, I'm thoroughly ruined. Not in the sense of being a committed flirt who was jilted in embarrassing circumstances, but irredeemably soiled. Therefore, waiting is pointless. Don't you agree, darling?"

A growl tore from his throat. Holly bit her bruised lip to keep from grinning, but she was most gratified when he lay back and shucked off his trousers as fast as he was able. "You win, love. Neither of us wish to wait. I am being selfish, not gentlemanly, in delaying the inevitable."

"You are a gentleman. Too much of one," she murmured.

"I can't promise to be anything close to that with you now." He was naked at last. Holly caught a glimpse of his proud member. Then he had her in his arms and rolled on top of her. This time, he didn't stop kissing his way down her navel. He continued straight down into her—

"Ohhh…" Holly arched off the bed. His finger slicked between her folds, followed by a quick invasion of his tongue.

"All right, love?" He grinned wickedly at her from between her thighs.

"Yes…I had no idea people did things like…what you're

doing now." Heat flooded her cheeks. This was so undignified. Still, she wanted more.

"You wanted to find out, my curious kitten," he chuckled, teasing. "Couldn't wait a few more days."

This was a side of Rey she wanted to see more of. "That's right. Show me, husband."

He delved inside her with commanding strokes. His tongue swirled around the sensitive spot at the apex of her sex. "Oh, yes. Oh, Rey." Syllables spilled from her lips in a jumble as he licked and sucked her with an intensity she had only vaguely imagined. Her body spasmed and she cried out.

"That was wonderful," she said dreamily. "But it wasn't anything like what I thought it would be."

"No?" Rey's smirk ought to have told Holly that she was being presumptive, but she was too blissfully happy to ponder its significance. "What did you think would happen?"

"I thought you would put this—" she fondled his arousal —"inside me."

He kissed her. "That is the traditional understanding of sexual mechanics."

"You mean, there's more?" Holly sat bolt upright.

Still, he hesitated. "Are you certain, love?"

"I have never been more certain in my life. I want you for my husband and I want you inside me. Today."

He groaned. "You'll be the death of me, minx. I can deny you nothing. Here. Straddle me like so."

Holly arranged herself over his muscular thighs, feeling shy and awkward. "Rey it hurt?"

"It might. A little. We'll stop if you don't like it."

"You keep reminding me of that. I'm starting to feel as if you don't want me." Horrifying thought.

But Reynard let his head fall back against the cushions and closed his eyes. "I do want you. More than anything in the world. I kissed you that way because when a woman is aroused, the act is less likely to hurt. I only want you to feel good, love. If anything feels wrong, tell me." She closed her eyes in what she hoped passed for agreement. He cupped her face. "Holly. Look at me. I want to see you when we come together."

Embarrassment flashed through her, unwelcome but real. Holly squeezed her eyes closed. "I can't."

"Dear heart," he rumbled in a voice so low she felt more than heard it. "You can."

She inhaled deeply and opened them. What she found seared her soul. Aching need and a vulnerability she never would have expected to find in a man, searching the very depths of her soul. Her awkwardness shifted form into a breathtaking feeling of power, both gentle and invincible. This must be what it meant to hold another person's heart.

"I'm ready," she whispered huskily.

He caressed her hips, guiding her lightly as Holly tested their physical connection and sank her hips down to meet his. The indescribable sensation concentrated in her sex, driving higher as he rocked forward at regular intervals to meet her. Rey's gaze never left hers. Holly gasped when it seemed impossible to stretch around him. A shudder wracked her body. Panting, she eased off and then tried again. An unfamiliar fullness pushed her to the limit. Tiny beads of moisture dotted Rey's forehead.

"Holly, love, you're so tight."

"Is that a good thing?" she whispered.

"Immensely," he grunted.

Holly found the maximum she could take him inside her and dared to peek down at their joined bodies. How thoroughly undignified to be spread open in her most private place; how utterly wonderful to see him buried within her. Satisfaction she had only dreamed of rolled through her as he lifted her hips and drove inside her again. Holly dropped her forehead to the hollow between his shoulder and his ear and moaned.

"Keep doing that," he half-begged, half-ordered. Holly decided that letting her husband command her might not be such a terrible thing after all. She shifted to meet his thrust. Pleasure broke through her in a wave. Each motion drove her higher until tension coiled in her low belly.

"Touch me the way you did before," she whispered. To her immediate chagrin, Rey rolled over and withdrew. Her mewling protest was silenced as he rose onto his knees behind her and hiked her bottom high. Holly found she rather liked giving into his control—especially when he slipped the tip of his cock up her center and inside with one smooth motion. "Oh, Rey, yes," she moaned. He rewarded her with a quick brush of his blunt fingertips over the apex of her sex. Holly's arms nearly gave out. An inhuman sound rolled out of her throat, half agony and half delight.

"That's it, Holly." He urged her on with tight, frantic thrusts. "Keep going, we're almost there..."

Almost where? She had just enough time to wonder before he swirled the needy bud at her core and Holly's whole body convulsed with pleasure. Her hips lost their rhythm. No matter—Rey clutched her body close to his and drove hard. New, softer waves rolled through her. Holly's hand mindlessly gripped and released the rumpled bedspread as though searching for anything solid to cling to.

Rey rolled onto his back, panting harshly. "Holly."

"Yes?" she murmured. Her head settled into his bicep. The fragrance of their bodies perfumed the air.

"I think we'll get on very well together as husband and wife."

She nuzzled close to him, feeling protected and safe. "I agree, husband."

Rey chuckled. The light filtering in through the fringed

red curtains dimmed and darkened. They lay together in the candle light, talking of nothing and everything, until Holly's stomach rumbled.

"I suppose we must go down for supper," he chuckled, running one flat palm over her protesting belly.

"How tedious," she complained. "Here. Behind the curtain is a bowl for washing. Amity said we might want it." Fortunately, the red wall hangings would conceal the fierce blush surely turning her cheeks red.

"Alas. We must keep up our strength to repeat this on our wedding night," Rey teased. He dropped a kiss on her forehead, then said, "After you."

Holly washed the stickiness from her thighs and passed a fresh cloth to him. Today she had left behind all things girlish and entered into a new phase of womanhood—and Rey Sharp had been the man to take her there.

※

Holly crept down the stone stairway confident in her ability to sneak up to her room before supper. With no wood to squeak in loud betrayal she was sure to make it to safety without—

"Holly?"

Or, perhaps not. Her face froze in a chagrined grimace. The ball of her foot was still poised on the last step with the hem tickling her ankle. There was an innocent explanation for wandering about in a night rail and man's dressing gown after tea and before supper, surely. Any moment now, her brain would produce one.

"Holly Mayweather, is that you?" Lady Stapleton's gray hair lent a sternness to her otherwise bewildered expression.

"I...ah. Yes. It is I, Holly." Abandoned, when she needed it most, by her wit. Her talent was for repartee. Without a foil upon whom to sharpen it, she was remarkably flat-footed. The two women stared at one another for a long moment of silence. Then, there was a scuffle of shoe leather on stone and a large, warm male form with which she had been very familiar, very recently, barreled into her. Damn stone for muffling Rey's footsteps until it was too late.

"Lady Stapleton." He bowed. The lady regarded them with bright, knowing eyes beneath two eyebrows perched in surprised arcs halfway up her forehead.

"Mr. Sharp." Whoever would have guessed that three syllables could convey so much meaning? "The entire house has been wondering where the two of you had sneaked off to." Rey's handsome features tightened ever so slightly at the corner of his mouth and eyes. A faint line appeared in the center of his forehead. They were the only indications of his concern, but in them, Holly read genuine worry. Why? They were to be married. It couldn't be that great a scandal to be caught spending a few hours alone with one's almost-husband.

Rey coughed. "I beg pardon, my lady, but half the house has no idea who I am."

"Everyone, however, knows who Holly is. By reputation, if not by personal acquaintance." Lady Stapleton's gaze settled upon Holly, and she swallowed. "My goddaughter has always possessed a magnetic kind of charm, which I see you have been snared by as well. I confess myself astonished that your mother's matchmaking efforts have borne fruit—possibly for the first time in her life." The lady winked conspiratorially. They were not in trouble. Holly relaxed and gazed up at her betrothed with open affection. His cravat was rumpled, his hair stood on end in odd places from where she had run her fingers through it, and he'd missed a button on his waistcoat. Despite this, she had never seen a more handsome man. It had nothing to do with fine clothes or an affected pretension of cutting intelligence. Rather, it was the soft shine in Rey's brown eyes that set butterflies free in her stomach.

Standing by Reynard's side made her feel complete. His protective presence let Holly be more herself than she had ever been in London.

Lady Stapleton's features rearranged into a stern expression. "I trust you understand that the two of you will be standing before Vicar Name in the morning. There will be no further delay. I pride myself upon being a lenient host, but I draw the line at ruining young ladies under my own roof."

"Understood, Lady Stapleton," Holly agreed. She caught Reynard's hand and wove her fingers between his. "We'll be ready first thing."

"Thank you. I want no scandals ruining my house party." Her expression darkened. "There have been quite enough close calls for one holiday."

"We shall see it through this time." Holly's belly flipped in her stomach as he raised her clasped hand to his lips and pressed a kiss to her knuckles. "You've no need for concern. I promise."

"I am glad to hear that." Lady Stapleton softened. She embraced Holly with one arm and pressed a kiss to her forehead. "It delights me to see two fine young people coming together. I wish you every happiness."

"Thank you, godmother." Holly accepted her affection with a grin.

"Now go, both of you, and get ready for supper. You shall have plenty of time to celebrate privately after the vows have been spoken. In the meantime, I ask you to present a proper front. For my sake. I won't have the Stapleton name associated with scandal."

"Of course." Holly glanced down. "I'd best scurry back to my room before anyone else sees me."

"Take the servants' staircase. No one will see you if you go quickly. Let's at least try to keep this as quiet as possible."

"Thank you, Lady Stapleton."

"Yes. You have our gratitude," Reynard added.

"Oh. One last thing, Holly. You received a letter this afternoon. I shall have the maid bring it to your room."

Holly glanced back over her shoulder. "That isn't necessary. I'll collect it at dinner." With a quick glance at Reynard, she continued on her way. "I can't imagine who might have written to me. All my friends are either here, or have abandoned me."

"Not all, it appears," Reynard chuckled. "Now go on, before you catch your death."

Chapter Eleven

The next afternoon, Reynard caught sight of his beloved as she came down the grand main stairway, and promptly swallowed his tongue. Their coupling had done nothing to slake his thirst for her. From the first moment he had laid eyes upon her, he had been obsessed with Holly Mayweather. Hell, it had started before that. The mere description of her had been enough to make him, an otherwise cautious chap, ask a complete stranger to become his most intimate acquaintance. Before he had even met her, Rey had felt possessive of this woman in a way he had never felt towards anyone else. Making her his had only reinforced the primitive urge he felt.

Perhaps that was why, when she descended the last stair and stopped short before the silver salver placed on the elegant console in the foyer, Reynard watched instead of greeting her. He was captivated by her and, deep down, knew he always would be.

Holly never glanced up. She scooped up the letter and broke the wax seal. Rey waited. He had been a spy, once, and observing Holly required no great effort. A moment of stillness. The self-possession not to react when her brows knit together over the bridge of her nose. Although he could not read the letter from ten feet away, he was close enough to overhear when she muttered, "Of all the presumptuous…"

If she cursed, it was too quiet for him to catch it. Intriguing.

Holly's chin jerked up. She hastily crushed the note and tucked the ball into a pocket accessed through a fold in her skirt. Well, he had earned his right to be in the Stapleton household through cunning and hard work. He would find a way to read the letter if it killed him.

It's not your concern, an inner voice spoke. But of course, it was. Was he expected to stand by while his wife pursued a secret correspondence with a man? While it had been difficult to make out, Reynard was convinced that the scrawled address had been a man's writing. He coughed. Holly started, then beamed up at him. "Darling."

It was almost enough to erase his suspicions. Yet there was a tiny tight crinkle around her eyes that belied her tension. There was a stiffness in her shoulder when he took her elbow, and her thoughts seemed distant as they walked in to dinner together. Mrs. Mayweather beamed at them and fluttered her handkerchief. He ought to feel nothing but satisfaction at Holly's winsome presence by his side. Lord and Lady Stapleton, the Mayweathers, and the Westons showered them with approval all evening.

Still, he could not relax. That crumpled letter in Holly's pocket haunted him. A deep urge to know its contents plagued him. What if their afternoon in the tower had been an act? Holly had seemed like an innocent, but what if she had been hiding her pregnancy by another man? Reynard wanted to trust her and yet part of him simply…couldn't.

That niggling twinge in his gut had saved his life too many times to count. He didn't dare ignore it now.

"Is something wrong?" Holly whispered after they had dined and were gathered in the parlor for post-supper games and drinks. She cradled a glass of mulled wine between slim, pale fingers.

"I might ask the same of you."

She stiffened. "What do you mean?"

"The letter. Who was it from?"

"No one." Holly dropped her gaze to the floor. "An old acquaintance from London. I don't intend to respond."

A fierce, possessive anger surged through Reynard's body. "What did he want?"

"How do you know it's from a man?" she asked querulously.

He glared at her. "You just confirmed it for me."

"I did not."

"I repeat, Holly, what does he want from you."

"Nothing you won't have by tomorrow morning," she teased, but it felt forced and hollow to him. Holly grasped his forearm and fluttered her lashes at him. Reynard shook her off irritably.

"Don't toy with me, Holly."

She pulled back. Her expression smoothed into a blank canvas. The only hint of emotion was the artificial upturn at the corners of her mouth. From across the room, one might mistake it for a young woman's joyful contemplation of her nuptials, but Reynard knew better. After a few minutes of stiff silence, she excused herself and left for bed.

Damn.

Finlay Weston caught Reynard's eye from across the room. They had not yet repaired their friendship—and if there was ever a moment when he had needed a confidant, it was now. He went to Weston's side and murmured, "Care to join me in the library for a brandy?"

As though he sensed the weight on Reynard's chest, Finlay nodded once. "Let me make my excuses to my wife. I shall meet you there momentarily."

In the dark silence of the library, Reynard helped himself to a drink, tipped it back, and drained it in a single swallow. The brandy burned a path down his midsection. He refilled it and settled into the leather club chair next to the dying fire in the large grate. Sitting was too restless, however. He got up and scanned the rows of bound knowledge, tracing the gilt spines with one blunt fingertip. Reynard paused before a book titled *The Love Sonnets of William Shakespeare*.

"Listen, Sharp, I owe you an apology." Finlay strode in, poured himself a drink and settled onto the leather sofa.

"No, Finn, it is I who must express my regrets," Reynard said ruefully. He left the book on the shelf where he'd found it. Words of heartfelt longing had no place in the world of aristocratic marriage. "You are right about Holly. She is a determined flirt and I was foolish not to see it sooner."

"Oh?" Finlay relaxed against the seat. "Do explain how you arrived at this conclusion when you were so recently praising her virtues."

"She received a letter this evening." He swallowed a gulp of brandy. "From a man. I surmise she has been in correspondence with him throughout our courtship, yet she never once mentioned it. How am I to trust a woman who conceals the truth from me even before we have spoken our vows?" Frustration had knotted his guts into a hopeless tangle. For the first time in his life, there was no clear path forward. He could not make sense of the facts before him to discern possible outcomes. The only one he could see was too terrible to contemplate.

"For a cool-headed military strategist, you seem to be conjecturing a great deal from a single letter," Finlay observed. He had kicked off his shoes and propped his stocking feet upon the butter-soft leather.

Rey smacked the bookshelf. The noise made his friend sit up straighter. "A fortnight ago, I believed I could make peace with a wife who did not love me as long as she did not embarrass me with a public affair. I find that is no longer the case." He shoved away from the shelves to pace the room. "I have developed…feelings for her. Now, I cannot bear the thought of another man's name on her lips, much less in her bed."

Finlay settled back down with a knowing chuckle. "Aha."

"What is that supposed to mean?"

"You've gone and fallen in love with her."

Reynard's heart pounded. Yes, he'd used the word as a term of endearment, and one half-drunk night he'd dared to contemplate the possibility, but to have gone and fallen head over heels with his own wife-to-be was a recipe for heartbreak. He knew better than to trust good fortune. "I have not."

Finlay smirked and swirled his amber drink. "There's no shame in it. Happens to the best of us."

"I tell you, I am not in lo…" Reynard choked on the word. "Oh, good god, you may be right."

"Told you." His friend chortled with irritating smugness. If it not for Reynard's dawning acceptance of the truth he might have protested further. He had crossed the Rubicon of smittenness and was deep into the territory known as hopelessly besotted. Somehow, he had never noticed the passage. "Didn't even see it coming, did you?" said Finn.

"No," Reynard replied ruefully. "Your complacent insights aren't exactly helping, though. What am I to do with a wife I cannot let go, and cannot accept unfaithfulness from?"

The naked anguish in his question knocked Finlay's smugness away. "Why do you assume Holly will betray you?"

Reynard gritted his teeth. "She is beautiful, wealthy and intelligent. I have nothing but scars, the promise of a tumbledown knighthood from our notoriously flighty Prince Regent, and the personality of a grumpy badger to offer her. I'd look elsewhere, too."

Finlay's feet found the floor and he came over to poke Reynard in the chest. "That is not what Amity says. She said Holly and you spent an intimate afternoon together, and furthermore, that she had never seen her cousin as happy as she was afterward. It doesn't sound to me as though she is pursuing an affair with another man. In fact," his friend continued without permitting Reynard to get a word in edgewise, "What you said the other day caused me to rethink the way we've treated Holly. Even Amity feels chagrined at how we failed Holly last fall."

"In what way?" Reynard asked, although he was too flabbergasted to decide whether he was asking about Amity, Finlay's change of perspective, or both. Fortunately, his friend answered all the potential meanings of his astonished question.

"Amity and I have both treated Holly as though she were nothing more than a foolish flirt with no thoughts in her head beyond who is marrying whom amongst the *ton*. Yet, when I reflected on Amity's first season, I came to realize how much Holly smoothed the path for us socially. She has a superb memory for faces and names. On more than one occasion she quietly steered us away from an unsuitable acquaintance. With Holly, I never had to worry that Amity would be exposed to the rougher side of city life. We were able to relax and enjoy our time in a way that would have been impossible without Holly's help."

"I could use that kind of insider knowledge if Prinny ever

comes through with granting me the living he promised," Reynard said ruefully.

"Exactly. And another thing," his friend continued. "Amity realized she used to judge her cousin for Holly's interest in frivolous things like clothing and dancing. Yet, left to her own devices, Amity would have made do with a few modest quality gowns. I encouraged her to spend whatever she liked after we were married, but years of poverty had trained her save at every opportunity. If Holly hadn't coaxed Amity into purchasing a full wardrobe, I expect the ton would have mocked her as a country bumpkin. Amity would have been mortified. Worse, if we are blessed with children, one day they would be seeking wives and husbands and our reputation might have one day impacted their happiness. Being on the wrong side of public opinion can have serious consequences for the entire family. Holly has proven her worth as a sophisticated navigator of social politics…on par, I should say, with your strategic skills at war."

Reynard said nothing, but drained the glass. "What you're saying then, is that we have all underestimated Holly."

"Yes. And I am certain that you are doing so now. Holly had many admirers in London. Probably some lonely chap penned a note wishing her happiness in the new year."

"I leapt to conclusions," Reynard said ruefully.

"Indeed."

"How do I—" He choked. Fix it? Stop the sinking feeling in his stomach that he had sabotaged the very closeness he desperately desired because he had been too afraid to acknowledge the gift Holly had given him without hesitation —the gift of her heart? "How do I make it up to her?"

Finlay clapped one hand on his shoulder. "Easy, mate. You grovel."

Reynard closed his eyes. "Anything but that." The twinkle in his friend's eye should have irritated him, but instead it calmed the stew of feelings Reynard didn't know what to do with. "Fine. I'll go and beg forgiveness for being a mutton-headed codswallop. I just need one thing." He reached past his friend's shoulder to slide one slim volume from the shelf. "A little help from Holly's favorite poet, the Bard himself."

Chapter Twelve

The morning of January fifth dawned gray and hazy—a fact Holly knew because for once, she was awake to see it.

"You, of all people, have no reason for wedding jitters," her mother noted sarcastically. Lady Stapleton had had a quiet word with her parents. There would be a wedding today. If Reynard did her the dishonor of refusing her at the altar again, Holly's father had informed her that was prepared to seek legal redress.

That meant a breach of promise suit.

Holly shuddered to contemplate it. She was ruined. An engagement was as good a marriage, in the eyes of society. A lawsuit would confirm her disastrous decision to the world. She would be forever relegated to living as a poor relation, forever dependent upon relatives to make her way in the world.

The alternative was to marry a man who didn't love her, refused to trust her, and hope that he might eventually come around to seeing her as an independent person with thoughts and feelings and friendships of her own. After hours of trying and failing to sleep she had pulled out the offending letter to read it one last time.

Dearest Holly,

I trust my letter reaches you in good health and much happiness. I wish I could say the same. I find myself friendless and exiled in Paris. I am indebted beyond hope. My heart has been torn into shreds by my lover, who has run off with my valet after bleeding me dry of coin. You may find it shocking that I speak frankly about them now, but do remember how I never concealed my interests in adventure and new experiences from you. I know you to be a sensible and sophisticated girl. I understand your good name has also been tarnished by the fallout of my disgrace. I can think of but one way to make things right. I write to offer you marriage. I can give you an impeccable lineage and title, whilst you bring funds sufficient to resolve my current financial predicament. I promise to give you an heir—or to claim any children you choose to get by another man. Everyone wins. Please say yes—I long to return home.

"Does he think me stupid?" Holly muttered angrily, crumpling the half-read letter in her fist. "My dowry would be spent within the month." Pickford offered nothing but a loveless marriage and a title, and it was all so he could save face and return to London. She had been so blind to his selfishness. Holly deserved her fate. Her mother had been right all along. When it came to marriage, it was best not to get one's hopes up. Take the best offer you could get, as soon as you could get an acceptable proposal, and be happy with it. It was a woman's lot to be useful only as a means of conveying wealth. Too late, she wished she had followed her mum's advice.

There were only two options before her. Accept her ruination and a life of dependency, or marry Rey. Her heart cracked. In an hour, the third and final wedding ceremony would force her decision. She couldn't bear the idea of living on her parents' goodwill, but the prospect of a marriage with

Reynard while knowing he did not and could not trust her was equally impossible.

Holly choked and dashed a tear from her eyes. She had never been one for tears, and she would not indulge them now, even on the bleak and cheerless morning of her wedding with the man to whom she'd given her heart, but who couldn't trust her with his.

※

Reynard understood that he had hurt Holly, but it wasn't until she stood before him, unsmiling, with deep gray smudges beneath her blue eyes that he knew how deeply. Her impish humor had dulled, while her gaze had sharpened to an icy glitter of anger.

The Stapletons looked on with steel in their gazes, as though they sensed something was off between him and Holly and were bracing for the worst. Lady Stapleton arched one brow at him. Reynard swallowed. The small book of sonnets made his jacket sag to one side. It barely fit in the interior pocket. The volume's solid presence gave him comfort. He had spent most of the night marking passages. Words of the heart had never come easily to him so he would borrow from Holly's favorite wordsmith, Reynard Shakespeare. Perhaps the man who shared his given name could help him rectify the mess he'd created for them both—if it came to it. He still hoped not to need the poetry. Yet Holly's serene expression caused a sinking sensation in his gut.

"For the final time, we are gathered to witness the union of Mr. Reynard Sharp and Holly Mayweather," spoke the vicar. He cast a gimlet glare at each of them before proceeding. Reynard nodded once, chastened. Droplets of sweat moistened his neck beneath his collar as Holly's chin rose stubbornly.

He was going to need the book.

"Do you, Reynard Sharp, take Miss Holly Mayweather to be your lawfully wedded bride?" The vicar had apparently dispensed with the lengthier version of the vows in an effort to seal the deal.

"I do," Rey replied, surprisingly calm even to his own ears. He was confident now. He had suffered a foolish, unwarranted lapse of judgment in accusing Holly of infidelity. Yet, she was here. She must have forgiven him. Her gown today was pale ivory with a blue sash and yellow and blue embroidered sprigs at the bodice and hem. Her bonnet was festooned with orange blossoms. Where they had come from in the dead of winter, he didn't know. But surely, they were a good sign?

"Do you, Holly Mayweather, take Reynard Sharp to be your lawfully wedded husband?"

He had a single moment of warning as Holly's gaze narrowed almost imperceptibly. "I do not."

A gasp rose in unison from the witnesses. "Not again," a woman groaned. Possibly Amity, or maybe Lady Stapleton.

"Yes! Yes, I may speak for my daughter, she most certainly takes Mr. Sharp for her husband, *don't you,* Holly?" hissed Mrs. Mayweather. She hustled down the aisle to her daughter's side. "You. Are. Compromised."

"I've been ruined for weeks, mother. I have one tiny shred of dignity left to cling to and I will not relinquish it simply because I am in danger of more people disliking me than they already do." A fire lit her from within. Reynard swallowed. Even Mrs. Mayweather looked taken aback. "I have done nothing—not one single thing—to earn the mockery and condescension you have shown me. All of you." Her gaze scanned the room before returning to her mother. "You raised me to seek the best husband I could hope for. From the time I was in the nursery you have taught me to evaluate a man by the cut of his waistcoat and the size of his purse, and not to let a deficiency of his character get in the way of an advantageous match." She paused for breath, inhaling so the tops of her luscious bosoms rose and fell, reminding Reynard of all the wonderful things they had done together during their lone afternoon of happiness. His heart ached that he might never see those perfect orbs again.

No. On second thought, it was not her bosoms he would miss. It was way they had pressed against him when her body was languid with happiness against him.

Mrs. Mayweather blanched. "Holly...I never once suggested you—"

"Stuff it, mum," Holly glared, then turned her fury on the man who was now striding up the aisle to meet his wife. "You too, father. You are as bad as she is in encouraging us to marry for status and money with no regard to happiness."

Mr. Mayweather stiffened. "Dearest, your mother does not deserve your reprimand. We found you a fine man, with whom you could be happy if you would give him half a chance."

"I gave him more than half a chance," Holly protested. Reynard winced to know what was coming. "Every person in this room knows Rey and I spent an evening together, alone, in the tower room. There's no need to act as if it's some great secret. My point is, I gave Rey my innocence, and yet the instant I received one simple letter he leapt straight to accusing me of infidelity." She waved the much-abused square of cotton rag. At this distance he could make out the scrawled signature. Lord Pickford.

"I suppose you want to read it?" she glowered, holding it out to him.

"No." Honestly, he didn't care. It could have been ten offers of marriage and it would not have bothered him, because Holly had given her heart to him, Reynard Sharp, bastard born and suspicious to the core, undeserving of her love but grateful to have it—if he could win back her trust.

Holly had shown him that hard-heartedness didn't come from an abundance of funds. It came from feeling too insecure to give freely from one's heart. His mother would have been appalled to see how he tried to guard himself from Holly's enthusiastic love. Rey had acted the same way his bastard father had toward Miss Sharp, the maid who had loved a broken man and been ground beneath his boot heel. That was why she had claimed the moniker that bound him to his sire. His father had chosen to harden his heart against the boy who bore his family name—Reynard—but the fact that they shared a name didn't mean he couldn't make a different choice in how he treated the love of his life.

"Changed your mind, now that I'm upset enough to call off our wedding for the last time, are you?" Holly mumbled. Her chin wobbled a though tears were about to fall. "I'll read it, then."

Each word she spoke drove home just how badly he had misjudged her. Holly's hurt came through with every syllable. When it was finished, she crumpled it into a ball. "I will not be honoring Lord Pickford with a reply. I wish someone, anyone, had informed me of his interests before I made an ass of myself before all London."

"Miss Mayweather, this is a chapel and you will watch your language," the vicar chided.

But Holly was having none of it. "Did Jesus not ride an ass into Jerusalem?"

The vicar blanched. "He did."

"If 'ass' is good enough for God, it is good enough for me."

Reynard chuckled. She was glorious in her fury—even when she turned it on him.

"And you, Mr. Sharp. I will not be marrying you. Your

offer is no better than this travesty." She tossed the wadded-up letter at his chest. It bounced off and fell to the floor with a scuffle. "I wish you every happiness."

Holly gathered her skirts and tried to march past him. But Reynard wasn't about to let her go that easily. His hand shot out as she passed by in a huff of hurt feelings and unshed tears.

"Wait," he said, catching her elbow. Holly froze at his touch. After drawing a long breath, Reynard began to recite:

When, in disgrace with fortune and men's eyes,
I all alone beweep my outcast state,
And trouble deaf heaven with my bootless cries,
And look upon myself and curse my fate,
Wishing me like to one more rich in hope,
Featured like him, like him with friends possessed,
Desiring this man's art and that man's scope,
With what I most enjoy contented least;
Yet in these thoughts myself almost despising,
Haply I think on thee, and then my state,
(Like to the lark at break of day arising
From sullen earth) sings hymns at heaven's gate;
    For thy sweet love remembered such wealth brings
    That then I scorn to change my state with kings.

"Sonnet 29," Holly said when he finished. Halfway through the poem she had begun to turn toward him.

"An ode to man's feelings of inadequacy and a reminder of how fortunate he is to have his lady's love." He untucked the book from his pocket and held it out. "When I read this verse last night I saw what I had not wanted to acknowledge. As I so often do when it comes to you, I set about making the worst possible outcome happen. Can you forgive me—again?"

Holly smoothed her gloved palm over the cover. "I don't

know. Memorizing a poem doesn't change the fact that you don't trust me."

"No. It doesn't. We would need more time for me to earn it." What could he say to convince her? "I was—am—terrified of losing you. Before this week, Holly, I thought it didn't matter. You would be an ornament to decorate my new living, should it ever come to pass, and we would live separately. But the more I came to know you, the more I realized I could never tolerate a loveless marriage. I don't care how unfashionable it is to be besotted with one's wife. I am in love with you."

Holly regarded him with wary hope. "What made you believe I wanted to live separately?"

"You don't like the country. You love city life. When and if the letter granting me a living arrives, I will need to spend a great deal of time overseeing repairs to the grounds. I may only be able to go to London a few times a year."

"Rey. I enjoy London, but it won't be the same as it was before I met you. I am not pining to return."

Dared he hope?

She traced the gild edging on the book's spine. "I expect you might want a wife's advice on furnishing a home. If I were to change my mind."

"If you intend to do so, please by all means get on with it," the vicar interrupted grumpily.

"Please, Holly. Be my wife. You can make me grovel every day for the rest of my life. After all, the course of true love never did run smooth." His hand found hers and clasped gently. After a minute, she squeezed his in return.

"I never had any intention of marrying him after he left, you know. It is one thing to have a friendly companionable marriage, but quite another to be purely transactional about the arrangement."

"I very much agree."

Holly flipped open to a poem, which I have not yet picked out, and passed the book to the Vicar. "Here, read this, please."

The vicar cleared his throat and began to read Sonnet 16:
Let me not to the marriage of true minds
Admit impediments. Love is not love
Which alters when it alteration finds,
Or bends with the remover to remove.

"Reynard Sharp, I consent to be your lawfully wedded wife."

A cheer went up from the back of the room.

"Shh!" the clergyman hissed as though worried they might yet jinx the ceremony before its completion. "I now pronounce you man and wife." He snapped the little volume closed and declared, "You may kiss the bride."

And with that, Holly and Reynard became Mr. and Mrs. Sharp.

Epilogue
SIX YEARS LATER...

"Do you remember the Twelfth Night ball when we were first married?" Holly asked. Humor touched her soft lips. Snowflakes glistened on her curls. Strains of a waltz floated out over the balcony and onto her creamy exposed shoulders.

"Yes." The evening had been out of a fairy tale. The bride he had not deserved to win had not left his side the entire evening. Their entrance to the Stapleton's ballroom had been their first appearance as husband and wife. Upon the announcement of Mr. and Mrs. Sharp a deafening cheer had nearly rocked the roof from its rafters. "You were the loveliest bride ever to blush her way through a crowd."

She chuckled. Puffs of her breath drifted into the cold air. "I was so proud to have the handsomest groom at my side."

He bent to press a gentle kiss to the pink, plump lips he had tasted every morning since. "And most devoted."

"I am a very demanding wife. Or was, until little Georgie and Charlotte came along."

It was his turn to chuckle. "What a pair of rapscallions you've given me." The towheaded, brown-eyed little scamps kept their grandmothers very busy indeed. His mother, now styled Mrs. Sharp and full-time resident of her own cottage at Kingscroft Tower, the property Prinny had finally gotten around to granting Rey a few months after the wedding, visited the house daily. To his great relief, the two women had gotten along splendidly. Holly had been so eager for a mother's approval that any mother would do. Even better, once she saw her place as chief irritant in Holly's life had been successfully contained, Mrs. Mayweather had changed tactics. Now she entertained herself by competing with Mrs. Sharp to see which grandmother could dote more on the grandchildren.

The country, it turned out, held more than enough intrigue and drama to keep Holly occupied between Seasons in London.

He tucked her beneath his arm as they shuffled down the snow-dusted path way. A bright moon illuminated the forms of Amity and Finlay Weston holding hands in the moonlight. Her last sister, Mary Anne, had married the fall before to a widowed vicar. The Mayweather family's many fruitful branches continued to expand apace. Amity liked to joke that Mayweathers would account for half the population of Herefordshire, after a few more marriages. The women remained as close as ever, especially with children born within a few months of one another.

"Speaking of our delightful offspring," Holly said with a smirk that crinkled the inner corners of her eyes. Rey knew now that it meant she was laughing at an internal joke and had come to love the sight. "Are you ready to add to our brood?"

"Already?" Two children in six years were hardly prolific by aristocratic standards, but Holly had decided to breastfeed George and Charlotte as infants. Children would come in good time, and they would be healthier by waiting. They had only recently begun to try for another babe.

"A midsummer babe, if the midwife's guess is correct. I had been holding onto the secret, just in case. I thought tonight was the perfect time to tell you."

"It is, love." He squeezed her hand. "Any time is the perfect time to tell me, but to be here, with your godparents where we were married makes it all the more special."

"I thought, if you liked the idea and if it is a boy, that we could call him Reynard."

Rey stilled. His natural father had passed two years ago. There had never been a reconciliation. Yet there had been a single, unsigned letter from his sire congratulating him on receiving a knighthood and Kingscroft Tower. Upon his death, an unexpected bequest to Mrs. Sharp had enabled her to purchase the cottage she so loved now.

"I know it has mixed meanings for you—" Holly said quickly. He cut her off with a kiss.

"It's perfect, love."

And it was.

❄

Cozy up to more swoonworthy Regency Christmas stories with ***The Duke's Christmas Scandal***. This short, steamy, Regency historical romance between a spinster snowed in with a secret duke is available to
Read in Kindle Unlimited

❄

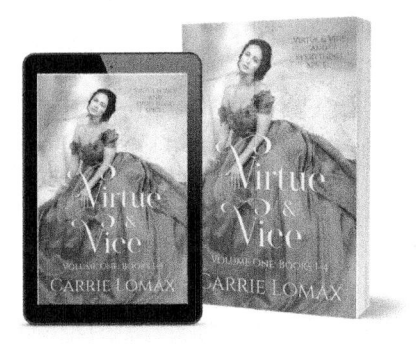

Dive into your next historical romance adventure with the Virtue & Vice series.

Set in Victorian London, the *Virtue & Vice* series is for readers who cried when *Harlots* was canceled, binged *Bridgerton*, and anxiously await the further adventures of *Miss Scarlet and the Duke*.

Belladonna is the morally gray heroine at the center of politics, society and crime. Hawke is the one person she cannot manipulate, charm, or blackmail into doing her bidding. Theirs will be the final entry in this seductive 7-book series, full of mystery and passion. The first box set volume contains the first four books of the series and a short series prequel, *Belladonna*.

Get 4 full-length romances, each with a happy ever after, plus a bonus prequel series starter. Save 40% off the retail price of each individual book when you buy Volume 1, available on any retailer.

You'll receive:
Annalise: A Spicy Enemies-to-Lovers, Virginity Auction, Victorian Romance (Virtue & Vice, #1)

Rosalyn: A Steamy Age Gap Victorian Romance (Virtue & Vice, #2)
Justine: A Steamy Victorian Masquerade Romance (Virtue & Vice, #3)
Cora: An Age Gap, Arranged Marriage, Enemies-to-Lovers Victorian Romance (Virtue & Vice Book, #4)

Ready to dive in?
Virtue & Vice Volume 1 **is available wherever eBooks are sold.**
Buy now on all retailers

Or get a 10-book mega-bundle when you buy direct from the author.
Get the Historical Omnibus

If you're not quite ready to commit, you can try the prequel for FREE when you sign up for my newsletter.

Author's Note

When I wrote this duet, it was to showcase a friendship between two very different women that is nonetheless deeply heartfelt and genuine. A wallflower and a socialite, cousins with every reason for resentment, find solace in one another and fall in love with unexpected men. I hope these novellas have warmed your heart this holiday season - or whenever you are reading them!

These stories are set during the golden era of English house parties. Visiting and hosting was a grand pastime among the upper class. Jane Austen wrote memorably of the country social scene - in fact, she was a gossip and a flirt herself with wonderfully scathing takes. Holly is loosely inspired by her witty letters to her sister.

I invite you to read another Christmas novella, *The Duke's Christmas Scandal*, an instalove historical romance between a secret duke snowed in with a spinster.

You may also enjoy my standalone novella with Max and Emma, *Married Off by the Duke*, an entry into the steamy Victorian world of my Virtue & Vice series. You can claim a free

AUTHOR'S NOTE

prequel when you sign up for my newsletter at www.carrielomax.com.

About the Author

Carrie Lomax is the bestselling author of historical & contemporary romance. She also writes angsty new adult fantasy romance under the pen name Joline Pearce.

Growing up rural Wisconsin, she spent a lot of time roaming the woods and fantasizing about new places. Adventures took her to Oregon, Michigan, and after a stint teaching in France, she moved to New York City, where she stayed for the next 15 years. There she acquired a pair of graduate degrees, a husband and a career as a librarian. An avid runner, reader, and cyclist, she lives in Maryland with two budding readers and her real-life romantic hero.

You'll find more of Carrie's books on her website, https://carrielomax.com, including:

The Virtue & Vice Series:
Belladonna (free prequel)
Annalise: A Spicy Enemies-to-Lovers, Virginity Auction, Victorian Romance
Rosalyn: A Steamy Victorian Age Gap Romance
Justine: A Steamy Victorian Masquerade Romance
Cora: An Age Gap, Arranged Marriage, Enemies-to-Lovers Victorian Romance

The London Scandals Series:
The Wild Lord
Becoming Lady Dalton
The Lost Lord
The Duke's Stolen Heart

Standalone Novellas
The Duke's Christmas Scandal
Twelve Nights of Scandal
The Spinster's Secret Scoundrel
Married Off by the Duke

Books by Carrie Lomax

Historical Romance

***Virtue & Vice* Victorian Historical Romance:**
Belladonna
Annalise
Rosalyn
Justine
Cora

Forthcoming in the *Virtue & Vice* series:
Isabelle
Rose
Jane

Novellas:
Married Off by the Duke (Virtue & Vice)

The Spinster's Secret Scoundrel (Cavalier Cove 1)
The Pirate's Stolen Bride (Cavalier Cove 2)
Secrets of a Duke's Heart (Wayward Dukes/Cavalier Cove 3)

BOOKS BY CARRIE LOMAX

The Duke's Christmas Scandal (Cavalier Cove 4)

Twelve Nights of Scandal
Twelve Nights of Ruin
(Christmas Duet)

***London Scandals* Regency Romance:**
The Wild Lord (London Scandals Book 1)
Becoming Lady Dalton (London Scandals Book 2)
The Lost Lord (London Scandals Book 3)
The Duke's Stolen Heart (London Scandals Book 4)

Contemporary series:
Say You'll Stay (Alyssa & Marc)
Say You Need Me (Janelle & Trent)
Say 'I Do' (Bonus Novella: Fiji Wedding)
Say You're Mine (Olivia & Ronan)

Fantasy Romance written as Joline Pearce:
Falling Princess
Eternal Knight
Queen Rising
Crimson Throne

Awakened series:
Sweet Briar: A Dark Fantasy Romance Sleeping Beauty Retelling
Midnight Deception: A Dark Fantasy Romance Cinderella Retelling
Queen Takes Rogue: A Dark Fantasy Romance

Visit www.CarrieLomax.com for details

Printed in Great Britain
by Amazon